ARROW THROUGH THE AXES

OTHER BOOKS BY
PATRICK BOWMAN

Torn from Troy: Odyssey of a Slave
Book I (2010)

Cursed by the Sea God: Odyssey of a Slave
Book II (2012)

Arrow through the Axes

the Axes

Odyssey of a Slave: Book III

Patrick Bowman

RONSDALE PRESS

ARROW THROUGH THE AXES
Copyright © 2014 Patrick Bowman

RONSDALE PRESS
3350 West 21st Avenue, Vancouver, B.C., Canada V6S 1G7
www.ronsdalepress.com

Typesetting: Julie Cochrane, in Minion 12 pt on 16
Cover Art & Design: Jake Collinge
Paper: Ancient Forest Friendly "Silva" (FSC) — 100% post-consumer waste, totally chlorine-free and acid-free

Ronsdale Press wishes to thank the following for their support of its publishing program: the Canada Council for the Arts, the Government of Canada through the Canada Book Fund, the British Columbia Arts Council and the Province of British Columbia through the British Columbia Book Publishing Tax Credit program.

Library and Archives Canada Cataloguing in Publication

Bowman, Patrick, 1962–, author
    Arrow through the axes / Patrick Bowman.

(Odyssey of a slave; book III)
Issued in print and electronic formats.
ISBN 978-1-55380-323-2 (print)
ISBN 978-1-55380-325-6 (ebook) / ISBN 978-1-55380-324-9 (pdf)

    1. Trojan War — Juvenile fiction. 2. Odysseus (Greek mythology) — Juvenile fiction. I. Title. II. Series: Bowman, Patrick, 1962– . Odyssey of a slave; book III.

PS8603.O97667A77 2014   jC813'.6   C2013-908267-0   C2013-908268-9

At Ronsdale Press we are committed to protecting the environment. To this end we are working with Canopy (formerly Markets Initiative) and printers to phase out our use of paper produced from ancient forests. This book is one step towards that goal.

Printed in Canada by Marquis Book Printing, Quebec

for my mother and father,
who never doubted I would finish

and for my sister Laurie,
who got me started

ACKNOWLEDGEMENTS

I want to thank my wife Barbara for keeping the wolf from the door while I was writing, and for letting me bend her ear about plot and character issues every night until she fell asleep. I would also like to thank my sister Laurie, who sorted out my characters' motivations for me, and whose observation that the dark ages of ancient Greece and the Trojan War might be connected was the basis for this trilogy. And perhaps most importantly, I would like to thank my publisher, Ronald Hatch, for having taken a risk on an unpublished writer who dreamed of a trilogy.

CONTENTS

CHAPTER ONE

The Curse of Helios

"SHE'S NOT NATURAL, no way. Shouldn't be following on us like that, no, never."

Frowning at the guttural Greek voices, I leaned on the stern rail and tried to recapture my thoughts. Safely away from the shore, the *Pelagios* was now catching enough breeze to leave a visible wake. Behind us lay the island where we'd stayed for the last month, held prisoner by an insistent wind that had risen to push us back each time we had tried to leave.

But our escape wasn't the main thing on my mind. It was what I'd learned, just before we'd pushed off the beach. My sister was alive! I felt a rare smile lift the corners of my mouth. For months I'd been certain Melantha was dead, killed by the same Greeks who had enslaved me. Now that I knew she was alive, I was going to find her.

Voices interrupted my thoughts again. "Never seen that before. Faster than us, sure. Maybe slower, maybe going another way. But following us? Never." I sighed and turned my head to see Lycos and Lycourgos, two of the younger Greek soldiers, gazing anxiously upward from the rear rowing bench.

Directly behind us, a small black cloud hung low in an otherwise blue sky, hiding the sun. Sitting idle at their rowing benches while we were under sail, the rest of the crew were muttering, casting anxious glances skyward.

Up in the bow, Lopex, commander of the Greeks, reached a decision. "Out oars, men!" he called. "Phidios, set a pace. Procoros, same direction." Waves began slapping at the hull as the oars bit into the water, but it quickly became clear that the cloud was keeping up with us. I peered up at it and shivered. Was I imagining things, or did the centre of the cloud look like a closed eye? I'd hoped that by escaping the island, we had also evaded its curse, but now, with the cloud above us, I knew with sick certainty that we hadn't.

Lopex was studying the cloud carefully from the bow deck. He gestured to Zanthos, who obediently twisted his steering oar in the water to take the *Pelagios* on a gentle turn to starboard. Not much, but enough that the wind could carry the cloud past us to port.

It didn't. As every eye on the ship watched, the cloud visibly changed course, tracking us. The ship began pitching more heavily, and I realized the wind was picking up, spume blowing off the tops of the waves.

Maybe the fates had already judged us. Perhaps what came next would have happened anyway. Just the same, Lopex's next move was exactly the wrong one. "Adelphos and Polites, furl the sail! Port side rowers, backwater on my signal! If we can't outrun it, let's see if it can turn corners!" He waved to Phidios, who immediately began the stiff-armed gestures to synchronize the new rowing pattern.

For a heavily laden ship, the *Pelagios* turned quickly, bringing us around into the wind, now rocking the ship with regular heavy gusts. "Both sides, standard row! Watch Phidios! GO!" Lopex roared over the rising gale. All eyes were turned upwards, mouths moving as each man prayed to his favourite god that the cloud would pass us by.

The gods weren't listening. Turning into the wind left us nearly motionless, despite the exertions of the sweating rowers, and the cloud caught up immediately. I held my breath, hoping it might yet blow past, but as it reached a point directly overhead, it stopped. The Greeks peered up fearfully as the cloud began to grow, filling the sky above us like the slow wingspread of a monstrous hunting bird. It spat a sudden torrent of hard rain at us, rain that stung as it struck.

As I clung nervously to the stern rail, watching Zanthos the steersman struggle with his oar, the men began clamouring even louder, their oars dropping unnoticed from their hands to foul the others.

Directly above us, the eye in the cloud was opening.

A furious orange light blazed down as though the sun itself was gazing angrily at us. The sun? The blood drained from my face as I realized whose eye was above us. I curled into a ball at the stern, hoping it would be over soon, damning the fortune that had bound me to Lopex. Why had I been permitted to learn that my sister was alive, only to be destroyed now by the wrath of Helios, god of the sun?

The cloud rumbled. A bolt of lightning, blinding white, leapt from the sky to strike the mast with a massive blast that battered my ears and left me deaf. In the moments to follow, hearing nothing, I saw the end of the *Pelagiós* and its crew as if watching a silent play. The mast had exploded like a pine knot in a giant's fire, spraying flaming chunks of wood in all directions. A ten-foot length tumbled backward and smashed into Zanthos as he struggled with his steering oar, ripping a gash across the side of his face and neck before smashing him through the rail into the water. The wooden spar that spread the sail was sent spinning into the forward rowers like a huge saw-edged discus, ripping through men and ship alike before escaping through the starboard railing. Lopex had his mouth open, still shouting orders from the bow but the rowers had given up, cowering in terror beneath their oars.

A second bolt of lightning smashed the bow like a Titan's club, shearing off three feet of the prow and leaving the hull open to the sea. Facing directly into the wind, the gaping hole instantly began taking on water. The bow pitched sharply lower and the men began leaping overboard, choosing Poseidon's unlikely mercy over the sun god's certain wrath.

Helios was not yet done with us. A third bolt struck the ship close by me at the stern. I could smell burning flesh and hair, and looked down to see my palms blackened, my arms and chest blistered as though the lightning's fire had travelled through the rail to reach me. The same bolt had somehow burst the ship along its keel, and as I stood on the stern deck the two sides of the ship slowly split apart like a giant clamshell, spilling spoils and despoilers of Troy alike into the sea.

The shock as I plunged into the cold water brought me back to the moment, the water excruciating on my scorched skin. I kicked frantically, struggling to remember the swimming lesson one of the Greeks had given me. As each wave held me briefly on its crest, I could see the heads of other men bobbing like seagulls as they struggled and drowned around me, surrounded by floating pieces of our shattered ship. More tongues of lightning flickered from the cloud, seeking out and striking the floundering men. A wave of salt water forced its way down my throat. Coughing and gagging, I began to slip under the waves, when something bumped the back of my head.

I twisted around. My healer's box! I grabbed at one of the handles, but my burnt palms were too weak to hang on. I threaded my arms through the thick rope loops, hoping they would hold. Another wave kicked me to its crest, and I saw Lopex nearby, struggling to climb onto a broken piece of decking before another wave swept it from him, dropping him into its trough, where he vanished.

My hearing was coming back. From all directions came gasps and shouts as the Greeks struggled and died, skewered by lightning bolts that hunted them down amid the waves. Overwhelmed by the horror around me, I hardly reacted to the discovery that my healer's box was riding lower in the waves. Exhausted, I tried to tug my arms from the handles.

Something was wrong. My arms were caught fast. I tugged harder but the rope loops had swollen in the salt water, tightening and binding me to the box. Packed with heavy clay flasks and jars and now full of water, it was slipping beneath the waves, pulling me down. I clamped my lips shut as I was dragged down, but in my exhaustion I couldn't hold my breath for more than a few moments, and it escaped from my mouth in a rush. I looked up to see the last bubbles of my breath, winking in the fierce sunlight as they spiralled toward the surface like tiny silver fish.

CHAPTER TWO

Saved from the Swells

THE PRESSURE TO BREATHE was overwhelming. I struggled to free my hands, to keep my mouth shut and to kick to the surface, but against my will, my mouth finally opened and my lungs tried to breathe salt water.

I coughed violently, my lungs reacting to the rush of water. I was going to drown. Mela's face flashed through my mind, and I felt a painful sting of regret, knowing that I would never save her now.

Something brushed my arm. As I turned, it hooked my armpit and began hauling painfully at me. Pulling me up! Nearly unconscious, I looked up, the light from the surface growing brighter again. My face broke the surface and I heaved in a giant breath before vomiting out a lungful of sea water.

Hands pulled at me from a boat, and I could feel someone cutting the rawhide handles of the healer's box. First one, then the second parted, and I felt it sink away from me. In my half-drowned state I almost thought I heard a girl's voice. Mela? I didn't know how that could be, but hearing her voice, I summoned the very last dregs of my strength to haul myself over the edge of the boat before collapsing, unconscious, in the bottom.

I was lying on something soft. A gentle voice was murmuring in my ear. "Please wake up. I'll care for you. I promise."

My eyes fluttered open. A girl was leaning over me. "Mela?" I mumbled. No, not Melantha. This face was rounder, with short brown hair around a darker complexion and a fawn's eyes. I tried to think, but my mind wouldn't focus. Finally I got it. "Phaethusia? Phaith?"

She smiled. "I couldn't let anything happen to *you.*" I tried to sit up but she pushed me back. "Rest. You've got very bad burns, and I think you swallowed some sea water." She looked contrite. "I'm sorry about your burns. I never thought father would do *that.*"

I fumbled with my thoughts. I had met Phaith once before, back on the island of Helios, during the month that we were trapped there. Her words reminded me of something. "That was his eye in the cloud. Your father is Helios, the sun god!"

She nodded. "Of course, silly. That's why his cattle are protected. But the lightning bolts were from Uncle Zeus."

"Then that was your voice I heard on the water."

"Of course. Who did you think? As soon as I saw what was happening, I set out in my boat after you."

Another thought pushed forward. "And the Greeks? The rest of the crew?"

"If they ate the cattle, they're dead." Her voice was suddenly flat.

Dead? I swallowed. Even as their slave, I had come to like many of them. They were nothing like the monsters we had been told of, back in Troy. If you didn't count Ury and his group, they'd been as decent and honourable as anyone I'd known in Troy. Deklah. Pharos. Wiry old Zanthos. I closed my eyes, feeling the sting of tears on my cheeks.

Phaith shrugged. "They deserved it. They shouldn't have eaten the cattle. I warned you."

I struggled to sit up but winced at the pain from my burns and lay back down. "Wait," I said. "What about Lopex? He didn't eat any. Or Pharos. Did you see them?"

She shook her head impatiently. "I wasn't looking for *them*. I came for *you*. I brought you back here to my island, safe. Aren't you grateful?" She drew back, frowning. "I'd hate to think you weren't grateful, Alexi."

"What?" I blurted, confused. "Oh. Yes," I added quickly. "I'm very grateful. Thank you." She was still sitting back, watching me suspiciously. "I'm just sad for my shipmates," I added.

Phaith stared hard at me. "Why?"

I looked at her in disbelief. "Why do you think? They're dead!"

She thought this over. "Yes. I see now," she said. "They deserved their deaths, but you miss them anyway."

I stared at her, disturbed. "Uh, yes." Just what sort of girl was she?

She glanced at the nearby window. It looked as though the sun was just setting. "Time for your medicine." She went into the other room and I took a look around. I was in a bed with a woven sheet over me and what felt like a straw-stuffed pillow under my head. Beneath the blanket I discovered I was naked except for a loincloth. My hands, forearms and upper chest were blistered and red, where they weren't black, and had been smeared with oil.

Phaith came back in and handed me a bowl. "Here. It's for your strength." The bowl contained some sort of unpleasant-smelling tea. It was bitter, but by taking small sips I was able to choke it down. The effort left me exhausted, and I fell asleep.

I stayed in bed for the next month, listening to the constant clatter of a weaving loom in the next room, wondering what Phaith could be weaving. I was terribly bored, but with Phaith's care and nightly tea, my burns were healing, the blackened skin flaking off in palm-sized pieces to reveal bright pink skin marked with a pattern of branching scars, as if the lightning had etched its image upon me.

What troubled me was that I wasn't getting any stronger. If anything, I felt weaker, especially in the evenings. By late afternoon I could stand up, but after dinner my strength fell away and I could hardly lift my head off the pillow.

"Hush, my dear," said Phaith when I mentioned it. "You were badly burned." She stroked my hair. "Let the medicine do its work. When you're better, we can have picnics together," she murmured. "When the sun isn't out," she added to herself.

That night I woke up to voices. Exhausted as usual by nightfall, I was barely awake, but it sounded like an argument in the next room.

"Father won't like it," said a voice. A girl, I thought. Not Phaith.

"He won't find out." That was Phaith.

I missed the first few words but caught the other voice saying ". . . inside forever? Besides, he'll get old."

". . . stuck here on this island with nothing but the cows and you!" That was definitely Phaith. "Why shouldn't I, if I want to?" she added, sounding sulky and defiant all at once.

As I lost my battle to stay awake, I thought I heard the other voice saying "What makes you think *he* wants to?"

By the next morning I'd forgotten about it. Phaith bustled around the room after bringing me a platter of figs and cheese, sweeping, straightening my pillow and tugging the bed further from the window, although it was already in a shaded corner. "Have to keep you out of the sun, don't we?" she murmured, glancing at the window.

That reminded me of the conversation I'd heard. "Phaith," I asked, trying to sit up, "was someone else here last night?"

She speared me with a glance. "What? Of course not." She busied herself with the broom. "Why?" she added, watching me out the corner of her eye. "What did you hear?"

"Nothing," I said quickly. "It must have been a dream."

She stalked over and pointed the broom handle at me. "*What did you hear?*"

I was still as weak as a mouse. "Well," I began carefully, "I thought I heard voices. One of them was yours."

"Voices. What did these voices say?" Phaith asked, her tone dangerously calm.

I frowned as if trying to remember. "Something about your father. And you being lonely." An inspiration came to me. "I understand — you're all alone on this island with only cows for company."

Her dark frown vanished like a shadow in sudden sunlight. "Oh, Alexi!" she exclaimed, dropping the broom and coming over to give me a wet kiss on the lips. "You *do* understand! I told her you would. You're going to love it here, I know you will."

She drew back to look at me, holding my shoulders with both hands. "That was my sister you heard. Lampethia. She lives here too." Her mouth twitched. "Well, not right here.

But on the island." Her lips pursed. "She won't stay with me. She sleeps outdoors somewhere." Phaith leaned closer. "She's crazy," she whispered. "Not like me."

Nearly a month later, my burns were healing well. Even Phaith couldn't find a reason to massage oil into them every day, but for some reason I was still too weak to take more than a few steps. "Don't worry, my sweet," she purred when I brought it up one evening. "Let the tea do its work." She stood up, taking my empty dinner plate. "I'll make you some now."

As she went off into the other room, there was a noise at the window. I sat up, listening, and the sound came again. "Don't drink the tea," it said.

"What?"

"Are you deaf? Don't drink the tea," the voice hissed.

"Why not?" I said, startled. "Who are you?"

"Did you say something, my sweet?" Phaith called from the other room.

"No, sorry," I called. "Just turning my pillow over." I turned back to the window. "Who are you?" I whispered.

A girl's face poked in through the window and turned toward me in the corner. "Lampethia," she said quietly.

I drew back in surprise. "Phaith's sister? Why shouldn't I drink it? I can't just —"

"Look, there's no time. Make up an excuse. Vomit. Whatever. Just don't —" Her face vanished from the window just as Phaith came into the room, carrying a bowl.

"Here you are, my sweet," she said. "Are you *sure* you

weren't talking?" she asked, looking at me oddly. "I thought I heard you. And look, you're sitting up."

I shook my head. "Not me," I said lightly. "Just banged my arm on the wall. I was muttering," I added awkwardly, rubbing my elbow.

She thrust a cup at me. "Here's your tea. Drink it down."

She stood nearby as I held it. "Drink it," she repeated, watching me closely. "Drink it now."

Suddenly I was suspicious. "I'm sorry, Phaith," I said, trying to come up with an excuse. "It's just that, well, this is really bitter." I smiled apologetically. "It's hard to drink."

Phaith put her hands on her hips. "What are you talking about? You drink it every night."

I nodded, trying to look contrite.

"Fine," she snapped. "I'll find some honey." She turned on her heel and stalked off to the other room.

I glanced around quickly for somewhere to dump the bowl. The window was too far. The chamber pot! I reached down and poured the bowl of tea into it, tucking it back with my feet as cupboard doors slammed in the next room. I had just pulled the blanket up when she came back in.

"I've found some honey," she announced. "I don't know why —" she broke off as she saw me lying down, the empty bowl on the covers. "What's going on?" she demanded, picking it up. "Where's the tea?"

"I, um, drank it," I murmured, trying to sound sleepy. She frowned. "You're right, I was being ungrateful," I added, hoping she wouldn't notice that the chamber pot had moved. She sighed and took the bowl into the other room.

The moment she was gone again, the voice at the window came back. "Not bad. Meet me out front at moonrise. Be quiet. She's a light sleeper." A rustle of bushes told me she had gone.

I lay on my side with my eyes closed, wondering how I could fight off the nightly stupor and stay awake until moonrise. I wasn't sure I even wanted to. If Lampethia was as crazy as Phaith said, sneaking out to talk to her would be a bad idea.

When Phaith came back into the room, I shut my eyes and pretended to be asleep. I heard her blow out the oil lamp, close the shutters and slip into the bed on the other side of the room. A short time later she began to snore. For some reason I was still awake.

In fact, now that I thought about it, I was feeling stronger, my nightly weakness gone. Nothing was making sense lately. The half-heard conversation a few nights ago. Phaith's reaction when I asked about it. My nightly weakness. I lay there, trying to puzzle it out.

Several hands — a Greek measurement of time, but I'd gotten used to it — must have passed before the cold white glow of moonrise appeared through the shutters. I hadn't been sure what I would do, but the moment had come. There was something wrong here, and the answers might just be outside.

I slipped the blanket off and swung my legs over the side

of the bed. Across the room, Phaith's breathing changed as my feet hit the floor. I waited until it had slipped back into a steady rhythm before straightening up. To my surprise, I stood up easily. I stayed still for a few moments, letting my balance return, before creeping to the doorway.

The shutters in the other room were open, and the moonlight cast a dim light through the room. Now I knew what Phaith had been doing at the loom every day. Nearly every piece of wall was covered with hanging tapestry. I crept over to the nearest but couldn't make it out in the darkness. Unhooking it from the wall, I wrapped it around my bare shoulders against the night chill, opened the front door carefully and stepped out.

A shape detached itself from a stand of moonlit olive trees nearby. "Didn't think you were coming," Lampethia said quietly. She glanced at my bare feet and loincloth, and the tapestry around my shoulders. "Nice. Now let's go before my sister wakes up."

I set off after her as she started to walk away but stopped after a few paces. "Lampethia," I called quietly. "Wait."

She turned impatiently. "What is it?"

"What's going on? Why should I go anywhere with you?" It was still early spring, and the chilly night air wasn't helping my temper.

"Look, you've got a chance to get away. Are you going to take it or not?"

"Get away?" I repeated, puzzled.

She walked back to me. "You mean you haven't figured all this out?"

I shuffled uncomfortably. "Well, I know that I've been taking a long time to get my strength back —"

"Totally missed the point, haven't you?" She shook her head. "Thought you were smarter than that, kid. Look, trust me or don't. But you'll wish you had."

She looked at the indecision in my face and grunted. "Okay. Walk with me. I'll answer your questions along the way, if they're not too stupid." She turned and set off.

I trailed behind her as we climbed out of the slight valley that the cottage sat in to set off through the rolling hills beyond. Despite her impatience, I noticed that she slowed down whenever I fell behind. My strength grew as we walked.

"Look at you," she said as I caught up. "Yesterday you couldn't get out of bed. Got it yet?"

I shook my head. "I don't understand. This strength — where did it come from?"

She glanced at me. "Wrong question, kid. You should be asking where your strength *went*."

I turned my head to look at her, thinking. The moon was well above the horizon now, lighting up her profile. She was taller than Phaith, her hair cut short and tied at the back. It looked practical. At the moment her thin lips were twisted in disdain.

I thought about it, not wanting to sound foolish. What did she mean, where had my strength gone? I was recovering from my burns, that was all. Or was it? I'd recovered from them a while ago, but my strength was still gone. Until tonight. Until —

"It's the tea, isn't it?" I blurted. "It was keeping me weak!"

Her glance was scornful. "Hades' holes, boy. You didn't notice?"

I blinked. How had I missed it? It was after dinner every day, after Phaith served me her nightly tea, that I became weak again. And the next day, I started getting my strength back. Gods, she was right. I'd been blind.

Lampethia sighed. "I suppose I shouldn't expect too much. You're only a mortal. And a boy, at that."

That startled me. "Mortal?"

"Our father is Helios. God of the sun. We're demigods. What would you expect us to be, geese?" She watched in amusement as comprehension flooded my face.

"So that's what happened with the cattle!" I exclaimed. "That was you!" She looked quizzically at me. "When they came back to life," I explained. "After the Greeks slaughtered them, the night before we escaped." Just before your father destroyed our ship, I could have added.

"Don't be a fool," Lampethia snapped. "My father's cattle are just hard to kill. But that's another reason you've got to leave now, before he sees you."

"Another reason?"

"Do I have to explain everything? Your biggest problem is that Phaith wants to keep you here."

"No, she doesn't," I interrupted. "She's just healing me. I don't think she even likes me."

Lampethia reached over and yanked away the tapestry I had wrapped around my shoulders, holding it up to the moonlight. "Open your eyes, boy."

Two people peered out at me from the cloth. One looked like Phaith, holding a baby sheep. The other was a boy, with straight black hair and a slim build. I leaned closer and realized with a shock that the boy was me. And what Phaith was holding wasn't a lamb. It was a baby!

Lampethia interrupted my thoughts. "Get it now, kid? Her other tapestries are all the same rubbish. She kept you weak, hoping you'd come around, agree to stay. She doesn't understand." She sighed. "Gods and mortals. It never, ever works. You'd get old and die. If you ever went out in the sun, our father would see you. You *really* don't want that. And one day Phaith would kill you by accident and spend a century grieving."

I nodded. "So that's why you're helping me."

She stopped short. "Get this straight, fleshling. I'm not helping you. I don't like mortals. I'm helping my sister avoid a bad mistake."

"How?"

"A ship beached in the north cove yesterday. You need to be on it when it goes." She gripped my shoulder painfully. "But here's the important part. *You have to be gone by sun-up.* My father didn't used to care if ships landed here for water, but since your friends pulled that little stunt with his cattle, he's been furious. If he sees a ship here, it'll be thunderbolts again. And when Phaith finds you gone," she added, "she'll head straight for our father."

Her words brought me back to the shipwreck of the *Pelagios*. Lost in my memories, I didn't realize that we were approaching the sea until the crash of waves alerted me. Lampethia pointed. "The cove is just over that hill. Remember: if that ship is still here at sun-up, you're all dead."

"Lampethia," I called as she walked away, and she turned back. "I know you're not doing this to help me, but thank you anyway."

Her thin lips twitched in irritation.

"Also," I added, "say goodbye to Phaith for me. I know she's lonely. Tell her I'm sorry I couldn't stay."

Lampethia looked at me for a long moment. "For a mortal, you're not so bad. I'll tell her." She turned and disappeared back down the hill.

To the east, a dim light was just beginning to mark out the line of the horizon. In a little more than a hand, the sun would rise. I had to convince these sailors to leave before then.

I crept down the hill to peer at them from behind a tuft of beach grass. There were only seven, lying in bedrolls beside their ship. Asleep on the sand, they reminded me of the Greek soldiers I had travelled with for the last two years. When I'd first met them, back in Troy, I had hated them, a swaggering gang of barbarians who had destroyed my city — and my family. But something had changed. I'd even come to respect Lopex, their leader and my master, a man who in some ways had reminded me of my own father. But that was before he had made a gift of me to Ury, the foulest man among the Greeks. I had felt betrayed. But since the shipwreck, I wasn't sure how I felt about him.

And then there was Kassander. He'd been my fellow slave, and had escaped just before we had set sail for the last time. I hadn't realized how much I missed his practical wisdom. My throat tightened at the thought that I would never see any of them again.

The horizon was growing brighter. I pulled free of my thoughts and got to my feet, but caught myself just in time. Walk into an encampment of sleeping Greeks? They'd cut my throat in an instant. I paused. What would Kassander have done? Remembering how he stooped and shuffled whenever the Greeks were around, I smiled. He would have made himself look completely harmless.

That gave me an idea. Re-wrapping Phaith's tapestry raggedly around my shoulders, I crept toward the camp, now much too visible in the pre-dawn light, and lay down on the sand an oar's length from the nearest sleeper. "Water!" I croaked.

No one stirred.

I tried again. "Water!" Still nothing. "In Poseidon's name, water!" I shouted.

That did it. The men sat up blearily, rubbing their eyes and looking around. I moaned again, clutching my throat for good measure. The men scrambled to their feet as they caught sight of me. I twitched feebly, trying to look weak and waterless. "Water!" I croaked.

It was working. Nobody had a sword out, and someone handed me a goatskin from which I did my best to drink thirstily. Finally I pulled it from my lips and looked up at a tall man with an air of command and streaks of white through his bushy hair. "Are you the captain?" He nodded. "Please," I gasped. "Leave this island now. Before sun-up."

A babble of questions from the men followed, but the captain cut it off. "All right, you crows, shut it." He turned back to me. "Who are you? Why should we leave?"

I glanced at the horizon. The sun would be up very soon now. I staggered to my feet, letting two of them help me up. "Look around, Captain," I said. "Green grass and rolling hills. Looks like pastureland for the gods, doesn't it?" I added, remembering what one of the Greeks had said. "That's because *it is.*"

They gaped at me. "Helios," I said. "The sun god. This is his island, for his cattle. If he sees your ship here, he will destroy you. With thunderbolts."

"Oh, really? Thunderbolts?" a thick-eyebrowed sailor asked, folding his arms. There was a skeptical murmur from the others.

Why couldn't they just believe me? "He did it to our ship.

The first bolt hit our mast. The second hit the rail near me. The *Pelagios* split apart and sank. The rest of the crew were killed by thunderbolts in the water. I was badly burned."

The captain shook his head. "Can't be done, chum. Our cistern is low, y'see? Today we'll water, perhaps rustle up some fresh meat. You're welcome to board when we leave. Tomorrow, I'd say, winds permitting."

"You're not listening," I said desperately, pointing. "The sun will be up soon. You have to leave now!"

One of the men frowned and held my outstretched arm by the wrist. "What's this?" he said, holding it up so the other men could see the new, pink skin on the underside of my forearm.

"Those are burn scars," said the sailor with the thick eyebrows slowly.

"Bad burns," said another, running a finger along the scars. He followed them up my arms and tugged aside the tapestry I had wrapped around myself. The men stared at the strange pattern of scars on my chest. "Take something fierce to cause these."

"Captain?" someone said uncertainly. "This doesn't look right. Those burns, that's not natural."

"He's right, Captain. I saw a man once, hit by lightning. It leaves its own mark on the body, just like this. Maybe we should —"

"Cast off," the captain whispered hoarsely, staring at my burns as if transfixed. The men looked at him uncertainly.

"D'you hear?" the captain roared. "I said cast off!"

The men turned as one and ran for their ship as the greedy fingers of dawn reached the hilltops behind the beach.

CHAPTER THREE

The Seer's Tale

THE MEN SWARMED up the stern boarding ladder with me close behind. Two steersmen headed for their oars while another two took up position at the bow. Unlike the *Pelagios*, which the Greeks had drawn up onto the beach each night, this ship had been left floating in the shallows, anchored to stakes pounded into the sand.

Someone threw off the loops around the stakes. "Push!" the captain shouted. Men heaved at the ship's four oars. It rubbed momentarily but slid free. The men continued poling us out until the water became too deep, and at a word from the captain, switched to rowing. As the ship slowly pulled away, the captain joined me at the stern rail and looked back at the island, still only an arrow's flight behind us. We both turned anxiously to starboard, just as the edge of the sun appeared over the horizon.

I held my breath. "What's next, then, chum?" the captain asked quietly. "Think we're in the clear?"

"I don't know. The sun was overhead, last time. It started with a small cloud behind us."

We both looked up. Aside from a few pink wisps near the horizon, there were no clouds in sight. The captain thumped the railing. "The *Sappho's* a good old tub, but she was never built for speed. Well, we'll just have to wait and see." He licked his finger and held it up. "Ruddy dawn. No wind. Well, let's be getting that sail up. Out past the roads, we might pick up a breeze." He clumped off down a walkway toward the centre of the ship.

We watched anxiously as the sun climbed, but no clouds formed to follow us, and no lightning bolts rained down. Around noon, the captain glanced around the still-clear sky and announced to the crew that, Poseidon willing, we had escaped.

The *Sappho* was a wide-bottomed cargo ship, very different from the streamlined *Pelagios*, my former master's ship. Both were about the same length, but the *Sappho* was at least twice as wide in the middle, and had no rowing benches. The front and back third of the ship were decked in the same fashion as the *Pelagios*, but instead of rowing benches stretching across the centre, it had two narrow walkways along either side, looking down into an open hold. The four oars I had seen earlier were all that it had — two at the stern, also used for steering, and two at the bow. Even before a fresh wind, the ship barely crept along, nothing like the high speed horse ride I'd been used to on the *Pelagios*.

The captain seemed surprised when I asked him about it later that day. "What do you think you're on, chum, a warship?" he asked, handing me a sailor's chiton from the hold. I began to reply but he kept on. "Not to worry. You'll get the hang of things, right enough. The *Sappho's* a cargo ship. Rowers would need food and water. D'you see down there?" He pointed into the hold, which appeared to be full of large metal plates. "Copper ingots. That's what we're shipping. If I had to carry a load of sailors, plus all that food and water, I'd lose half my cargo space and most of my profit. Can't have that, can we now?" He winked at me.

"Now it's your turn, chum. Who are you? And what in Poseidon's good name were you doing on that island?"

I wasn't about to admit to a shipload of Greeks that until recently I'd been a Trojan slave, or the son of a Trojan healer. I fumbled for an answer, when it came to me. "My name is Alexi. I was a sailor on a cargo ship. The *Gala*," I added, thinking of Phaith's cow.

"*You're* a cargo jack, chum?" the captain blurted, startled. "Sorry," he added. "I'm right sure you're a fine sailor. It's just that most sailors are a little older."

"It's okay," I said. "I'm short for my age." It had been several years since Lopex had enslaved me back in Troy, although I hadn't been counting birthdays. I'd grown taller since then, and was at last starting to show a wispy beard, but I was never going to be as tall as the Greeks around me.

"Well, then," said the captain, rubbing his hands, "welcome to the *Sappho*, Alexi. An able sailor is always welcome. Now just what could have brought you to that island?"

"We were sailing from Ismaros," I began.

"What cargo?" the captain broke in.

"Uh — grain. Millet," I answered. "We were caught in a storm. It blew us off course, until our navigator had no idea where we were on his charts."

"Navigator?" he said, puzzled. "Your captain didn't do his own navigation, then?"

"Uh, no," I answered, thinking quickly. "He used to, until his eyes went and he couldn't read the maps." The captain nodded sympathetically.

"We drifted until we landed up on that island." I skipped the details. "A girl there warned us that the cattle belonged to Helios, the sun god. But we had unfavourable winds and couldn't get off the island for a month. Eventually, the men sent out a hunting party and slaughtered three of the cattle."

"Wait a moment," said the captain. "Why didn't you eat your cargo?"

I paused, confused. "Your cargo," the captain repeated patiently. "The millet. Why in Hades didn't your crew eat that?"

I was beginning to regret not staying closer to the truth. "Of course. I mean, of course we did. But a lot of it had been spoiled in the storm. When we opened up the sacks, most of them had mildewed."

The captain looked at me suspiciously. "I don't know, boy. If the choice was stealing a god's cattle or taking a spot of mildew with my corn, I know what I'd choose."

"Um, right. It was really mildewed. Our storesmaster nearly threw up when he opened the first sack."

"Hold up a moment, boy. Now you're saying you had a storesmaster too? Just what kind of cargo ship was this?"

I floundered for words under his hard stare. Suddenly his expression changed. "It's all right, Alexi. You're running from something, aren't you?" He gestured around the ship. "Half the men on this ship, they're running away. Tell me the truth. You're no cargo jack, are you, chum? You don't have the hands, for one thing. You were on a warship, weren't you?"

I hesitated. "You're right, Captain. It was a warship. But what I said about the island was true. If you'd stayed, you'd be dead by now."

The captain looked at me closely. "If you say so, chum. Sounds to me like you've left off as much as you've told. But we've all got our secrets. Once you get to my age, you'll have worse!" He thumped my back playfully. "Next time, start with the truth. It'll get you a lot farther."

That reminded me. "Captain, can you tell me where we're headed?"

He looked at me in surprise. "I didn't say? We're headed for Mycenae. The citadel has a standing order for copper, and they pay a fair price. Well," he added, "as fair as anyone."

Mycenae! I had to grab the rail. Taking passage on a Greek sailing ship was risky enough. Walking into the city of Agamemnon, the powerful Greek king who had led the war against Troy, would be madness.

Freed from Phaith, my strength had returned quickly, and I began to help out on board. I was surprised to realize how much I had learned from watching the Greeks, and soon found myself striking and raising the sail, tying it off, and once, as the youngest and lightest, shinnying up the mast to free a rope that had become wedged. There were differences, of course. The *Pelagios* had always sailed directly before the wind, rowing whenever it wasn't just the right direction, which was most of the time. With only four rowers, the sailors on the *Sappho* were much more skilled at using the wind, angling the sail and working their steering oars to adjust their direction. Still, there were at least ten days when we went nowhere, either because there wasn't wind to stir the sail or because it was too far off our course. On such days, we returned to the beach from the night before, if we could, and the sailors stretched a sail and sat in its shade, doing what sailors did best — grumbling.

"Not keen on shipping into Ceeni, I can tell you. Ugly city. Not as bad as Sparta, mind. Place got worse when the queen took up with that Aegisthus fellow, after King Agamemnon died," grumbled one, a pinched-looking older sailor named Kleos. "Whole city's like an armed camp now. Guards everywhere."

I listened carefully. I'd had time to think about it, and although the idea of a visit to Mycenae was still daunting, the largest of the Greek city-fortresses would have taken the eagle's share of the slaves from Troy. If I was going to find my sister, Mycenae was the place to start.

"It ain't right, what happened to the king, neither," muttered Deipyros, a thin man with bristly grey hair and a nose like a bird's beak. "They say he died in his sleep. Survived the ten years before Troy, then died the night he comes home?" He shook his head. "Not likely."

"Maybe it was seeing his Queen Cly again that did it to him," suggested Kleos, to laughter from the others.

"Maybe," Deipyros muttered darkly. "Maybe that's just what happened."

"That reminds me," said the captain, turning to me. "Once we put into Mycenae, Alexi, where are you bound? We've been short a deck hand this season, and you know your way around a rope. There's a berth on the *Sappho* if you want it."

Sail with the *Sappho*? The thought was appealing — but no. My sister was alive, and I was going to find her. Even if it meant entering the fortress of Mycenae. I shuddered. If they realized I was Trojan, I'd be enslaved again in an instant, if they didn't just kill me as a runaway.

"I'm sorry, Captain," I replied, shaking my head. "I have to find my sister, and Mycenae is a good place to start."

"Your sister?" he asked, surprised.

"Um . . . yes. She was kidnapped from our village, three years ago. By bandits." I felt sweat on my forehead as I realized how close I'd come to giving myself away, but the captain just shrugged. "Have it your way, chum. It's a big world."

It was a late afternoon about a half month later that the crew furled the sail for the last time, and the four oarsmen carefully manoeuvred the ship up against the deep water docks at Tiryns, the port of Mycenae. Three other ships were moored along the two jetties, loading or unloading. The port, one of the sailors told me, was a day's ride from the citadel of Mycenae itself, which had been built on an inland hill to protect it against invasion by sea. "'Course, it means all the goods has t'be carried in by carter," he added. "Can't see how it's worth it, myself." I could have told him. If Troy hadn't been built so close to the coast, the Greeks might never have defeated us.

The ingots in the hold were flat copper sheets stretched out like ox hides, but with odd bronze loops in the top two corners. The next morning I saw what they were for. Two sailors on the pier threw strong hooked ropes down into the hold, as two more sailors below hooked each ingot by the corner loops so the sailors above could pull it out. A further two passed a pair of stout poles through the same holes to carry the ingot to a waiting row of donkey carts.

"Clever, eh, chum?" the captain remarked. "For eighteen seasons we manhandled ingots up a ladder from the hold. The foundry master at Alashiya, he came up with those loops two seasons past. Saves us a packet of work, I can tell you."

The carters, a group of greying old men, sat in silence in their carts on the jetty as we loaded the ingots, grunting when a cart was loaded incorrectly. It was around noon, with the last ingot loaded, that the captain finally hopped onto the lead wagon and gestured for me to join him. At a nod to our driver, the cart train moved out.

Perched on a hill, the citadel was visible from far off. Home of King Agamemnon, Mycenae was known throughout the lands of the Greeks and well beyond, to Troy and even Egypt, as the seat of a mighty empire. But from a distance, it was just a squat, unpleasant-looking fortification that spread across the hilltop like a fungus.

As the cart train climbed the hill, the details came into view. Close up, it was just as unpleasant. The squat, grey wall must have surrounded the original city, but Mycenae had grown past it, low buildings sprouting like mushrooms outside. Back in Troy, the main entrance had been through two proud wooden gates, a lion's head carved on one and an owl's on the other, symbolizing a balance of strength and wisdom. Mycenae's main entrance was a squat, overhung passage that our cart could barely pass through, two scowling lions glaring down at us as we approached.

The captain, who had been relaxed for most of the ride,

nudged me anxiously as our cart rolled to a stop. "Best to sit quiet here, chum. Let me do the talking, okay? And whatever you do, don't look them in the eye." I looked up, startled, as two armoured men approached. Bronze battle axes hung from leather thongs at their hips.

"State your purpose," one said, his voice flat. I bit my tongue. We were leading a train of carts loaded with copper ingots. What did he think we were doing — invading?

The captain kept his voice calm. "Seventy-three copper ingots from Alashiya for delivery to the royal foundry."

The guard said nothing, walking slowly down the wagon train, pausing occasionally to rap on an ingot before returning to us. He stared coldly at me. "Your name?"

"He's my assistant." The captain answered swiftly. "He helps with the unloading."

"Your name?" the guard repeated.

"Alexias," I replied, keeping my gaze down. "Alexias of Heraklion." My father had been from there, a safely Greek city on Crete.

The guard reached over and squeezed my right forearm painfully. "You help unload?" he asked. I nodded but said nothing. Compared to the captain's rock-hard arms, mine were as limp as rags.

The guard stared at me for a few moments longer before straightening up, apparently deciding not to press the point. "Deliver your goods and get out," he said, making a dismissive gesture. "We don't like strangers."

Our carter, who had sat impassively through the inspection, flicked the reins. The rest of the cart train followed us as we moved off through the gate and into the city's market square. Inside the square, armed guards stared down from the wall, while others strode through the marketplace, pausing to peer into market stalls or stare at the customers. On the far side of the square, the palace towered two stories above us, its windows scowling down at the square.

The captain turned to me. "Those city guards, they'll throw you in the dungeon for the wrong glance. Since the business with King Ag a few years ago, the whole city's been like that. Queen Cly and her new lover, they trust nobody. And they're very suspicious of strangers. But you probably got that, chum!" He punched my arm playfully.

"King Ag?" I asked carefully. "I heard he had died in his sleep."

Instead of answering, the captain hopped down as the cart train came to a halt at one side of the market square beside a building with wide double doors. "Ho! Foundrymen! Copper ingots!" The doors swung open and several burly men came out to unload.

The captain and I moved out of the way. "Don't believe everything you hear, Alexi," he said quietly, glancing around. "My cousin, now, she's a washerwoman at the palace. After King Agamemnon died, Queen Cly got two slaves to move his body. She had them killed, but not before they told someone what they'd seen." He lowered his voice even further.

"King Ag's body wasn't in bed at all, no matter what they said later. It was in the bath, all cut up. Think about that, chum."

"She killed the slaves?" I asked, startled.

"Well, sure, but that's not the point. Someone killed King Agamemnon. With an axe." He peered at me more closely. "What's the matter, Alexi? You're looking pale."

If someone had killed King Agamemnon, he deserved it, as far as I was concerned. But could my sister be in there, with a queen who killed her slaves? I had to get in and find out.

"Have you ever been inside the palace?" I asked.

"Me?" He seemed surprised. "Never. Nobody gets in without an invitation." He gestured toward the palace's main gates, across the market square. Two sharp-eyed guards were interrogating everyone who approached.

The captain sighed. "Palaces. Places of lies and deception, where every shadow hides an axe, chum. Now, the sea, it's unforgiving, but if you can read the signs, you always know where you stand." He stopped and looked at me. "Have you reconsidered berthing on the *Sappho*? She's a tight ship, and you've got the makings of a good sailor."

I shook my head with honest regret. "I wish I could, Captain, but I've got to find my sister."

"Well, I can't say as I like your chances, but I admire your spirit." He held out his hand and I shook it in the Greek style, locking thumbs. "Fair winds, Alexi."

"Fair winds, Captain."

I spent the afternoon wandering the cobbled streets of the

city, wondering what to do. Guards were everywhere, staring hard at me as I passed and chasing me off if I stopped to rest. The whole city was alert and suspicious, just as the sailor on the *Sappho* had said. How could I get into the palace in a city like this? Hungry and disheartened, I wandered all afternoon and into the evening, watching the streets empty. Shortly after sunset, I curled up in the doorway of a cordwainer's shop and fell asleep, expecting to be awakened by the dawn light.

I awoke instead to a poke in the ribs. "You there! Are you alive, or did they dump another *nekros* on us?" I opened my eyes to see a shaggy man in a filthy, half-tied loincloth looking down at me. Around us were stone walls, and a stone ceiling overhead.

I sat up, alarmed, and winced at a painful throbbing from the back of my head. "Where am I?"

The man glanced behind me. "You hear that?" he asked. His voice rumbled as though he'd been eating gravel. "Sailor boy here doesn't know where he is." There was some rough laughter. I twisted around to see a half-dozen men sitting up against the far wall, most of them as scruffy as the man standing over me.

"But I fell asleep outside last night," I said slowly.

The man smirked. "Isn't that nice. The guards love curfew-breakers."

I stared slowly around the room, wincing again as the movement hurt my head. "This is a dungeon, isn't it?"

He looked at me in mock surprise. "Naw, you've got it all wrong. This here is more what you call a correctional. People with bad attitudes come here until they cheer up."

So I was in the dungeon. "How do we get out?"

"Well now, as to that," the man began, "you've got your three options." He held up fingers as he spoke. "One, you can get pardoned, if the queen changes her mind. Two, you can get punished. That gets you out, if you survive. Or three, you can be put to death. Lots of people get out on that one." He leaned in closer and stage-whispered: "Now if I was you, sailor boy, I'd try for number one."

I lay back, rubbing my head tenderly, until a thought struck me. "The queen? We're in the palace?"

The man glanced at his friends. "Doesn't miss a thing, does he?" Turning back, he gestured around at the stone walls. "Welcome to the palace, sailor boy."

There was a moan from the corner near the door. A short, rounded man with a receding hairline was sitting up. "It's happened again," he was saying. "It's a portent, I'm telling you. Something's going to happen. A man doesn't have the same dream night after night for nothing. Got to mean something."

I winced. His voice was grating and nasal, digging into my head like a pick. The other men groaned. "For Zeus's sake, Krython, shut up about your dream already."

"But it's the same dream again! I pluck some grapes and squeeze them into the queen's goblet. Doesn't anyone know what it means?" He caught sight of me. "You there. Don't recognize you. What's it mean?"

I groaned. "How should I know? If I'm lucky it means you're leaving."

"Do you think so?" he said, turning to me hopefully. "Palace wine steward is an important job, you know. Dionysus knows how they've been getting by without me."

"Okay, fine," I groaned. "It means you're getting out. Now leave me alone." I rolled over and pressed my hands to my ears, just as the wooden door to the cell swung open.

"Krython?" said the guard. "Krython, wine steward?"

"That's me," said the round man, struggling to his feet. "What is it?"

The guard looked him up and down. "The queen has pardoned you. Come with me." Krython scampered through the door, which banged shut behind him.

There was a momentary silence, and then all the men began talking at once. "Pardoned! Did you see that? He was pardoned. Right there, it was, sure as grapes."

The man next to me stood up and pointed at me. "*He* knew," he said, his voice unsteady.

The other men started in. "He knew?"

"He said Krython was leaving."

There was a pause.

"He did?"

"Heard him myself. 'Means you're leaving,' he said."

"Perhaps he's —"

" — a seer! Right here with us!"

"A seer? Don't be daft. What's a seer want with a dungeon? He'd be off seeing in the palace, that's what."

As the others murmured uncertainly, one man broke away and squatted beside me on the stone floor, a shaggy man with dark eyes. He reminded me of Ury. "Listen up, you," he said roughly. "I had a dream. I was carrying bread for the queen, but black birds came down and ate it all. Three nights, I've had that same dream. Tell me what it means."

I looked up at him, my head throbbing. "Leave me alone. It was just a guess."

"A guess?" he growled, winding his fingers through my hair and yanking my head from the floor. "Guess again, sailor boy."

"Let go of me! I don't know!"

He shook my head, making the pain worse. "Yes you do. Now tell me or I'll hurt you."

I glared at him. "Fine. It means you're going to die. Now will you let go?"

He let go of my hair and leapt back, black eyes staring. The other men had fallen silent. "Did you hear that?" someone breathed. "Arkesilios is going to die!"

I glanced over as I heard scuffling. The men had scrambled away to the farthest corner of the dungeon and were peering at me anxiously.

"He could have told him more gently."

"You'd think a seer would be more careful."

I winced. "Look, I didn't mean it. I've just got a bad headache. I'm not a seer, okay?"

The men mumbled amongst themselves. "Says he's not a seer."

"But they do that, don't they? All the good seers say that."

"The Pythia at Delphi, they say she doesn't know what she's saying either. Doesn't even know her own name, some days. The gods speak through her."

"And she gets terrible headaches, they say."

"Headaches?" The men turned as one to look at me. "There's your proof, right enough. He's a seer, all right."

I winced and rolled the other way. They'd figure it out.

And so they did, but not the way I'd expected. Three days after I'd been thrown into the cell, the guard walked in again. "Arkesilios?" he demanded. "Arkesilios, baker?"

The ragged man who had confronted me unfolded his long limbs and stood up. "That's me."

"Come with me."

"Have I been pardoned?"

"Not quite. You're being executed tomorrow." Two more guards came through the door behind the first, and the three of them dragged him away.

The other men turned to look at me, awe on their faces.

"Predicted it, didn't he?" someone whispered. "Told you he was a seer."

After that, the other men left me alone, carefully shifting to the opposite side if I approached. At least nobody else asked me to interpret their dreams.

CHAPTER FOUR

Escape from Mycenae

I SPENT THE NEXT three days staring at our cell door, trying to find a way out. The time was interrupted only by the occasional delivery of brackish water, which we drank from a common bucket, and a single meal a day, usually a hunk of mouldy cheese and some stale bread, most likely leftovers from the kitchen, tossed through the door onto the floor. At least, with the other men afraid of me, I was able to get my share of the meal without fighting for it.

Around mid-afternoon on the fourth day, the chance of a way out arrived. I was curled up in a corner, resting, when the door opened and a short, fussy-looking man with thinning hair came in.

"I'm looking for the seer." His eye fell on me. "Are you he? Come with me." He grabbed my arm and hustled me out. I didn't know what was going on, but it was getting me out of the dungeon.

I was taken up a stone stairway and through corridors, the fussy-looking man leading the way. "I am the palace chamberlain. The queen heard of a seer in the dungeon, a young man who could interpret dreams. Have you spoken to royalty before? No, of course not. Bow for a count of three. A deep bow, mind. Call her 'Your Majesty.' And for the love of Hera, don't interrupt. And leave a goodly silence after she speaks." He ran a nervous hand through his hair. "What else? Oh, a hundred things. I can't possibly teach it all. You'll just have to do your best."

We arrived at a room with a bed and a table. "Here is your room. This slave will help you wash and dress," he said, gesturing at an old woman who had followed us in with a folded tunic in her arms. "You will stay here until the queen summons you." With a last, disapproving glance at my sailor's chiton, now filthy from my stay in the dungeon, he turned to go.

"Wait!" I called out. He turned, frowning. I wanted to tell him that I wasn't a seer, but stopped. That would land me back in the dungeon.

"Well?" he asked, tapping his foot impatiently.

I hesitated. "Um — how long will it be before the queen asks for me?"

He sighed heavily. "I'm sure I don't know," he said, sounding frustrated. "Maybe this moment. Or days. And the queen doesn't *ask*. When she wants to see you, she commands." He turned and trotted off, looking anxious.

I wasn't eager to be washed by an old slave woman, so I asked her to step outside before stripping off my tunic. I thought furiously as I washed. Somehow, I'd gotten myself into the palace. Here was my chance to search for my sister! Cutting the wash short, I threw on the clean tunic and stepped out. I'd been ordered to stay where I was, but that might mean days of waiting. I was here now and wasn't going to waste the chance.

"Sir?" the old woman was standing outside the door, looking anxious. "Sir can't be planning to go out like that, surely?"

I looked at my chiton. "Why not?"

She glanced up and down the corridor. "If sir will just step back in for a moment?" I let myself be led back into the room. She untied the fabric and let it fall, leaving me unexpectedly naked. "Not to worry, sir," she said as she took the sponge and scrubbed at my face, "I've seen more skin than a cartful of tanners, young men and women both, sir." She clucked her tongue as she dried me off and draped the chiton around me again, tugging a corner over my shoulder. "Now just stand still, sir, this needs a proper pin," she said, shaking out the remnants of the knot I'd used and replacing it with a large bronze pin at my shoulder. "There. Now if we just touch up sir's hair, sir can go out looking like a free man."

"What do you mean?" I asked, startled.

"Well, sir," she said, giving my hair a vigorous brushing, "the way you had your robe tied, and your hair and face, anybody might take you for a street urchin, or a slave. We wouldn't want that, would we now, sir?"

While she showed me how to arrange my robe in proper court fashion — "just so as those folk at court don't think any the less of you, sir, which they'll do if you give them half a reason, that they will" — I realized she might be able to help me.

"How long have you been a . . . a . . ."

"A slave, sir?" she finished. "May the gods love you, there's no harm in saying it, sir. I was born a slave in this very palace under good King Atreus himself, so I was, and been a slave to his son, King Agamemnon, may the gods give him peace. And now, I'm in service to that wife of his, Queen Clytamnestra too, that I am, sir."

"Then you must know most of the slaves here in the palace, do you?"

She scratched a few grey bristles on her chin. "Can't say as I know them all, sir, but I know a goodly number, and all the upstairs."

"Have you ever seen a slave girl, maybe a few years older than me? Straight hair, grey eyes? She'd be tall, and slender."

The old woman scrunched up her wizened face as she thought. "Well, sir, most slaves are slender if we're not downright skinny, and that's a fact. The palace doesn't feed us to fatten us up, no sir." She looked at me shrewdly. "This slave girl, she could almost be a relative of yours with that hair and eyes, but never if she's tall, if you'll forgive me saying so. When would she have come into service at the palace, sir?"

"Around the time that King Agamemnon came home from the war, a few years ago," I said.

She shook her head. "Can't say as I can think of anyone, sir. But I'm in the upstairs, we don't mingle much with the downstairs folk."

"Downstairs?"

"You know, sir, the cooks, the washerwomen, the grinders, labourers and such. They don't dare come up to this level, they'd be beaten if they did, and that's a fact. You'd have to go down to speak to them, sir. There's a slave down there as might know, I've met her a time or three. She's a bit crazy, but she sees everything, she does, and she'll tell you if you ask, but you have to listen hard, sir. Don't let her tell your future, though, she'll try but she's always wrong. Just go down to the kitchen and ask for Cass, they'll know who you want."

I followed my nose to the kitchen, wondering why that name sounded familiar. Even inside the castle, guards were stationed at points along the hallways, watching me carefully as I passed. I tried to look like I knew where I was going, praying they wouldn't ask.

"Cass, sir?" mumbled a slave girl carrying a net of onions over her shoulder, avoiding my gaze. "That way, sir." Still looking down, she flung her arm toward a side room with a leather sheet for a door. I walked in to see someone sitting at a table, shelling pea pods from a gigantic earthenware pot. Her hair, knotted and filthy, hung over her face. A voice came from beneath it. "You've come. I knew you would."

I stopped in my tracks. Where had I heard that voice before? She husked another pea pod and brushed her hair away from her face, revealing smooth cheekbones and full lips. *Crazy Cassie.* The daughter of King Priam of Troy. I'd last seen her on the streets of Troy, the day before the Greeks took the city. I took a half-step back.

"I said you would live," she said reproachfully. "Not that anyone listens. My own nurse forced me to switch robes with her on the voyage here. I said she would die, but she wanted to be the princess. And when we landed here, they killed her. She should have listened. And just three days ago I said the serving *krater* would crack. But did they listen? Of course not. And the stew was spilled."

"That's great, but I've got —"

It was like trying to stop a flood with a twig. "I told them," Cassie went on. "But nobody listens. Find the one who rows to the fore." She grabbed my arm and stared into my face. "The one who rows to the fore. He will find her. Would you like a pea?"

"What?"

She held up an open pea pod, the smooth peas lying inside. "I eat a lot of them," she added. "They're good for the complexion, they say."

Feeling overwhelmed, I accepted one gingerly.

"Like piglets in their sty, aren't they? I always think so," she said, running her finger gently along the pod. "Now she dreams of the son she nursed, returning as a viper, ready to avenge. But she will not believe me, as you will not. That is my curse. I knew the sand would blow in the master mason's eyes and he would drop his brick. But that is my curse, always to know, never to persuade."

I listened as she babbled, looking for sense but finding none. Even back in Troy she'd been crazy. Apparently, captivity hadn't helped. I backed away and bumped into someone.

"Alexi!" I spun around to see the chamberlain, somehow looking annoyed and anxious at the same time. "There you are. Come on. The queen will be furious! You've kept her waiting, I can't think how she'll react. I've searched the whole palace. What are you doing here? And with the downstairs, too." He glanced at my robe as he hustled me up a flight of stone steps. "At least you're properly tied off. I won't be disgraced on your appearance."

I followed him breathlessly. What had Cassie been talking about? I shook my head, trying to clear it, as the chamberlain led me around a corner and into a small room. Several masks hung on one wall, and a carved wooden thunderbolt stood in a corner. "Now wait right here. You can't go in yet." He scurried across the room and peered between two large wooden doors on the opposite wall.

I felt queasy. What could I possibly tell the queen? I was no seer. But if I said so, I'd be back in the dungeon in an instant, or worse. It didn't sound like the queen took kindly to people who wasted her time.

For some reason, my old master Lopex came to mind. I still wasn't sure how I felt about him, but remembering him talking down a mutiny after the storm, or rallying his men in Hades, or after the ship eaters, was inspiring. If he were here, he wouldn't even hesitate. Lopex would do whatever it took. I drew a deep breath, just as the big doors swung open.

The room was what the Greeks called a *megaron* — a large, long room with pillars down the sides and an open hearth in the middle. Before each pillar stood a broad-shouldered guard in full armour, a huge Mycenaean battle axe hanging at his waist. At a nod from the woman on the throne at the far end, those giant blades would hack me to bits. Walking past those silent guards, I felt like a wooden arrow, threading my way through a forest of axes.

The chamberlain bowed as we approached the throne. "Your Majesty," he said, "may I present the seer who, with the gods' help, will interpret your dreams." As I did my best to mimic his deep bow, I caught sight of a slender, sulky young woman with blond hair draped over her black robe, sitting on a padded bench to the side. The queen's daughter, I guessed.

The queen was a strikingly handsome woman with a strong jaw, clad in a *himation* of brilliant yellow trimmed with purple. Her gaze flicked toward me for an instant. "He is late. And too young."

"I have seen dreams from Sparta to Athens," I said quickly, naming the only other Greek cities I could think of. "Your Majesty," I added, more slowly, "permit me to see yours."

The queen returned her gaze to me. "You forget your place, seer. But you are well travelled for one so young." She looked at me shrewdly. "What did you think of the city of Sparta, where my sister dwells?"

I swallowed. All I knew of Sparta was that Helen, the Greek princess who had caused the war, had come from there. "Sparta?" I said, trying to sound confident. "An ugly city, Your Majesty. And too many Spartans."

There was a gasp from the chamberlain, but the queen threw back her head and laughed. "I have often said the same thing to my father," she replied. "Very well, seer. You may hear my dream."

She leaned forward on her throne. "Tell me. What does it mean when the queen of Mycenae dreams of having an infant, but when it is brought to her to nurse, it is a snake? What does it mean when, instead of nursing, the snake bites her, drawing both blood and milk? Interpret for me, seer."

I hesitated. "The meaning is complicated, Your Majesty," I began uncertainly.

"Here we go." The bored-looking younger man draped across the throne next to the queen's spoke up. "Next he'll say it could mean many things. Get rid of him, Clam. He's boring."

The queen turned on him angrily. "I told you not to call me that in public, Aegisthus," she hissed. "And someone whose dreams are only of his own pleasure will never value their deeper meaning. Be silent." She turned back and gestured for me to continue.

Definitely not someone to cross. But what could I tell her? Any answer would do, if it sounded believable. The queen frowned as I hesitated.

Wait. What had Crazy Cassie been babbling? Something about a viper, buried in that stream of nonsense. That might work. "Your Majesty," I said quickly, as Aegisthus began another loud yawn, "I know what it means. You dream of a son. He returns."

I froze as I realized I had no idea if she even had a son. Could this prediction possibly make sense? But her response was clear. "My son?" she blurted, stiffening.

Aegisthus sat up on his throne. "What's this?" he asked. "A son? You didn't tell me you had a son." He frowned. "Sons take revenge. Continue, seer."

The queen gave a nervous laugh. "A son? Don't be silly," she replied quickly. "As I told you, my son Orestes died many years ago. He is no threat to you now. The seer is mistaken." She waved me away with the back of her hand. "Leave now."

Aegisthus began to object even as I edged toward the door. As I passed through it, I glanced back to see Aegisthus and the queen still arguing. Over in the corner, the sulky-looking blond girl in the black robe was sitting bolt upright, staring straight at me with wide blue eyes.

I wasn't sure what my status was at the palace any more. Was I still a guest? Would the queen ask me to interpret more dreams, or would she throw me back in the dungeon? It seemed wiser to stay out of sight, so for the next month, I skulked through the palace, interrogating any slaves who would answer, scavenging meals from the kitchen and returning to my room at night. The chamberlain, it seemed, hadn't been given any instructions, and wasn't about to throw me out on his own. Meanwhile, the old slave woman, Arsinoe, continued to change my wash water and bring me a clean chiton every day, but her attitude had changed.

"Can't see what you're spending so much time with the downstairs for," she said, her tone reproachful. "Just mindless drudges and grinders, they are." She gave the comb a painful tug as she ran it through my hair. "Stand still now, or it'll hurt worse. They're not like those of us above the stairs."

She pulled away and looked at me. "You're not one of them barbarians, are you?" she asked, sudden suspicion in her tone. "I've seen you speaking to them in foreign." She put down the brush and wrapped the chiton around me, scratching my shoulder with the pin. "We don't think much of foreigners around here."

I looked at her, startled. It was true, I'd been speaking to the Trojan slaves in Anatolean, the language of Troy. I resolved to try harder not to raise suspicions, not realizing that it was already too late.

It was two nights later that it happened. I'd spoken to most of the slaves — at least, the ones who had enough spirit to reply, for many didn't — but none of them had news of my sister. As usual, I had scrounged a meal from the kitchen, not wanting to show myself in the official court dining room.

I was in bed when I heard men shouting in the corridor. Someone ran heavily past my room, then several others. More shouting. I threw on my chiton and crept to the door. I was unlacing the leather catch when there was an urgent tapping on the far side. Puzzled, I pulled the door open a crack. A figure in a black robe covering head and face pushed it open and swept into the room.

The figure shut the door and turned to me, casting off the hood. By the light of her lamp, I could see the face of the black-clad young woman who had been sitting at the side of the throne room when I had read the queen's dream.

"Listen," she said urgently, her blue eyes fixed on me. "I am Electra. Daughter of King Agamemnon and Queen Clytamnestra." She held up a finger to hush me. "You have to leave the palace immediately."

I frowned. "Why?"

She gestured behind her toward the door. "Do you hear that?" In the corridor, men were shouting.

"My mother and her lover" — her face contorted at the word — "well, better that you don't know. But the palace guards are arresting everything that moves, especially young men. It won't be long before —" she broke off as heavy foot-steps halted outside my door. She darted to the corner and hid behind a hanging tapestry as the door was kicked open.

"There he is," said a quavering voice. "Right there, don't say I didn't tell you. Been asking a lot of nosy questions, he has." Two hulking guards with torches marched into the room. Behind them, pointing angrily at me, was Arsinoe, the old slave woman.

"Think you're so grand, don't you?" she said, scowling at me. "Talking all foreign to the drudges, asking about a special slave, getting the downstairs all upset." She turned to the guards. "Doesn't know how to tie a proper chiton, either. There's plenty that's strange about him, and no mistake." She sniffed. "Might even be a foreigner."

The guards pushed past her into the room and grabbed me by the shoulders. "The captain wants to see you," said one. "As for you, old woman," he added over his shoulder to Arsinoe, "you did right to tell us. Now be quiet." As they began to pull me toward the door, Electra stepped out from behind the tapestry.

"Stop! Where are you taking him?" she asked coldly.

The two guards halted, and Arsinoe turned pale. "Your Highness!" said one of the guards, bowing. "We were just bringing this foreigner —"

Electra cut him off with a glance. "He is not the one you seek."

"But —" Arsinoe began.

"How *dare* you question me, slave?" Only someone born to power could produce that tone of voice.

The guards bowed again. "Sorry, Your Highness. Very sorry," they mumbled, backing out quickly. Finding herself suddenly alone before the princess, Arsinoe bowed. "The same goes for me, Your Highness," she added. "Very sorry, I'm sure. All a mistake, this was." She bowed once more and darted out the door.

Electra turned to me. "The captain of the guard won't be put off so easily. I'll make this quick. There's a donkey and cart waiting in the stables. Ride the cart out of the stable, across the courtyard and straight through the south gate, as hard as you can. There's no guard there. Once you're safely outside the wall, follow the south road to the port." She thrust a jewelled bracelet into my hand. "This will buy you passage on any ship." She tugged me toward the door. "To reach the stable, go left to the end of the hallway and down the stairs. Follow the stone corridor to the doorway at the end, and cross the courtyard to the stables." She tugged the door open and peeked into the corridor.

"Wait," I said, suddenly suspicious. "Why are you helping me?"

She bit her lip, looking down. "You've heard about my father, the king?"

I nodded.

"He didn't die in his sleep. I've lived under the same roof as his murderers for two years, praying that my brother would return to avenge him. You gave me hope that he was coming. Thank you." To my astonishment, she came over and kissed my cheek before peeking out into the hallway again. "The way is clear. Go. Quickly, before the guards return. Remember, don't stop. Ride out of the stable and through the south gate as fast as you can. Quickly, before the guards think to search the stables." She pushed me out of the room.

Slightly dazed, I followed her instructions to the courtyard, guided by the light of flickering hallway torches, ducking out of the way as armed guards ran past. There was no moon, but by the faint glow of starlight I could just see the stable across the courtyard. It was as black as tar inside, and I found the cart only by walking into it.

Remembering Electra's instructions, I climbed into the cart and tried to make the donkey move, slapping the reins across its back as the carters did. Reluctant to leave its warm stable, it wouldn't budge. Feeling desperate, I was forced to climb back out of the cart and pull the donkey behind me, hauling it roughly by the reins.

As I approached the south gate, I stopped. Something felt wrong. As I hesitated, someone ahead of me cleared his throat. Peering into the moonless dark before me, I could just make out the outline of a pair of armoured shoulders in the starlight. A guard was standing in the very centre of the gateway.

How had Electra gotten this wrong? I couldn't sneak past him, and there was no way he would let me take a donkey cart out in the middle of the night, even if he hadn't heard the commotion. At the moment his back was to us, but he might turn around at any instant. Even in the near blackness, he could hardly miss us.

I put down the donkey's reins, praying to whoever the god of donkeys was — Poseidon? Dionysus? — that he would stand still, and ran up to the guard, keeping myself between him and the cart.

"Come quick!" I said as I approached, panting as though I'd been running hard. The guard spun about. "It's the palace ... the queen ... something terrible has happened! The captain of the guard ... he asked for you ..." I grabbed his arm as if to tug him back to the palace with me.

Even the most suspicious guard couldn't ignore a summons like that. He barely glanced at me before setting off at a run across the courtyard toward the palace. I followed him for a moment but fell back and made my way back to the donkey, still standing patiently off to the side, and led it out quickly through the unguarded gateway. After bringing it safely out of sight of the castle, I climbed onto the seat at the front of the cart and flicked the reins again.

Once again, the donkey didn't move.

I tried again, flicking them hard enough to hit the creature's back with a snap. It rolled one broad eye back at me but didn't move. What magic had the carters used? I couldn't walk the cart all the way to the port. Frustrated, I leaned forward and gave it a hefty kick.

That worked — just. With a resentful glance at me, it broke into a half-hearted trot. It took me some time to learn to control it. If I tugged on a rein to turn its head, it seemed to go the other way out of spite. Nonetheless, after a little while, by yanking hard on the reins, I could almost make it do what I wanted.

The city of Mycenae had leapfrogged the original city wall, and it took me a while to find the south road in the maze of streets. Eventually I found one that looked about right. With an effort, I hauled the donkey's head around to turn us downhill to follow it.

There were no sounds of pursuit behind me, but it seemed smart to put as much distance between me and the palace as possible. I wondered whether I'd been smart to take Electra's advice and flee. I'd done nothing wrong, but by now the guards would be sure I had.

I rode for what felt like a couple of hands, turning once or twice as I thought I heard sounds behind me but seeing nothing. The landmarks still weren't looking familiar, even with the light of a now-risen quarter moon, but at least I was getting away from the palace. At last, as I noticed the donkey's head and my own dipping further and further, I decided to stop and let us both sleep. Stopping, at least, was something the donkey was happy to do.

I turned around and climbed into the back of the cart, intending to curl up under a horse blanket I'd seen there. As I tugged on the blanket, my hand brushed something. It was a hand, and it twitched as I touched it.

CHAPTER FIVE

Confronting the Furies

STARTLED, I LEAPT BACK, almost tumbling out of the cart before catching myself and jumping down into the road. I waited for a moment but whoever it was didn't even sit up. Approaching the cart carefully, I peeked over the side to see a figure lying under a blanket. My momentary fright passed, and I felt a rush of anger. "Who are you? What are you doing there?" I demanded.

There was no answer. Whoever it was didn't seem dangerous. I reached in and yanked the blanket away, revealing a young man a few years older than me, curled in a ball on his side. He made no attempt to pull the blanket back.

"Who are you?" I repeated, puzzled.

The figure mumbled something and curled up tighter.

"Look, you're in my cart. Answer me or get out."

The figure did neither.

I scratched my head. He was quiet now, but pulling or prodding might provoke him. Besides, in the darkness he could have a whole butcher shop's worth of knives with him. "Okay. Stay there. I'll sleep down here." I crunched downhill along the gravelled cart track a short distance, but at a sudden thought, turned to creep quietly back past the cart to find a place to bed down. Whoever my strange passenger was, if he came for me in the night he'd head downhill. I hoped.

But when the sun woke me the next morning, he was lying just as I had left him. Despite the cold night he had made no effort to pull up one of the other horse blankets. I fumbled the anxious donkey out of its harness and watched it trot off to the nearby stream for a drink. Without the donkey to hold it up, the cart tilted forward on its two wheels to lean on its shafts.

There was a noise behind me. The young man in the cart was stirring, his eyes open. In the daylight, he looked about ten years older than me, wearing a well-made chiton. He turned his face toward me, revealing a high forehead above large blue eyes. His expression was oddly blank.

"Time for answers," I said. "Who are you? And what are you doing in my cart?"

He looked at me calmly. "They're gone now. We're safe." His voice was as expressionless as his face.

"Gone?" I asked. "Who?"

"*Them*." He shuddered. "They come at night. But they won't, not now."

Great. My passenger was crazy. "Who are you?" I asked, trying another approach.

He seemed to think about it for a moment. "Orestes."

Orestes. It sounded familiar, but I couldn't think why. At least he didn't seem dangerous. As I pondered what to do, I thought of my old master Lopex. "Dump him," he would have advised. "He'll slow you down. If the guards come after you, they'll find him instead."

I shook my head angrily. I didn't want to hear from my old master, even in my memories. But . . . it was true. If I dumped this man into the road, from the way he was acting, he probably wouldn't even get up. I reached for the cart shaft to tip it back on its two wheels, but he stopped me with a single word. "Please."

Angry with my own weakness, I let the cart shaft fall. "Fine," I said gruffly. "You can ride with me down to the port. After that you're on your own."

I re-harnessed the donkey and set it plodding with another kick. We hadn't been travelling for long before I realized something was wrong. With the sun above me and to my right, this couldn't be the south road to the port. We were going east! In the darkness, I must have taken the wrong route from Mycenae. There was no way we could go back now. We'd just have to take our chances heading east.

Around noon, the road snaked into a valley of overgrown olive and date trees. Nearer to Mycenae, there'd been a few farmers tending their crops, but further from the city, the orchards began to look wilder and overgrown, apparently abandoned. Orestes had said nothing all morning, staring blankly at the overgrown fields and orchards around us from the back of the cart, mumbling incoherently if I asked him anything. Now, with the midday sun beating down on us, we were going to need water soon. "Gods, I'm thirsty," I muttered.

A moment later there was a nudge at my elbow. Orestes was holding out a goat skin. Water! I snatched it up gratefully and took a lengthy drink. "Why didn't you say you had this?" I asked, passing it back, then paused. "Do you have any more?"

He turned and tugged aside a jumble of horse blankets. I stared in surprise. The messy heap had concealed several more goatskins of water, a few wrapped packages, a walking stick and a sword. I unwrapped one of the packages to discover a bundle of greasy cooked sausages, a hunk of dark cheese, and two smaller packets of dates and almonds.

This hadn't been thrown together at the last moment. Assembling all this had taken time. I looked up to meet his calm blue eyes. "Where did you get all this?" I asked.

"Electra," he said calmly.

"What?" I blurted. "Electra? Why would she do that?"

The sound of her name seemed to energize him. He sat up. "To eat," he said simply. "After I escaped."

I'd meant to ask "why would she do that *for you*," but part of his answer caught my attention. "She planned your escape?"

He nodded placidly and gestured at the blankets. "She hid me."

"In the cart?" I asked. "But you'd be caught there."

He paused. "Someone would try to drive the cart out, she said. She said to be ready to take the cart out myself, once the guard caught the driver."

I didn't notice that I'd dropped the reins. The donkey ambled to a stop as I twisted around. "She expected that?"

He nodded innocently. "She said he wouldn't see me at night."

My breath came out in a long hiss. She hadn't been helping me at all. She'd been setting me up! She'd expected me to drive right into the guard, after promising me there wouldn't be one. Once I was caught and dragged off, my passenger could drive right out the open gate. The guards would stop searching, especially once they found her bracelet in my tunic.

The *Sappho's* captain had been right — palaces were places of lies, where axes lurked in every shadow. I should have been furious. Somehow, though, I couldn't help being impressed. Electra had taken me in completely. The only thing she hadn't anticipated was that I would escape too.

"Okay," I said, thinking hard. "So Electra helped you escape. Why?"

For the first time, a calm smile touched his lips. "She's my sister."

I could have slapped myself. That was why I recognized his

name. Orestes was the name of the son the queen had spoken of, Electra's brother. I turned to him. "If you were escaping, what from? What did you do?"

The slight smile fell from his lips. "Nothing," he said, his voice flat.

"Nothing? Was that why the guards were running around last night? That doesn't sound like nothing."

"Nothing," he repeated flatly. "They said it was all right."

They again. "Who?"

He glanced around. "*Them.* But they won't come after us."

"Who? The guards? Why not?"

He looked at me in faint surprise. "The guards? Of course they will." He paused. "Oh yes. But *they* won't," he said, with an odd emphasis. "That's all that matters."

I sighed. He'd gone back to crazy again. I wasn't going to get any more answers from him right now.

It was getting too hot to travel, and from the way his hooves were dragging, the donkey badly needed a rest. I yanked the reins to steer it off the road and into the vine-draped trees, planning to pull us into some deeper shade, but as we rode further into the grove I spotted a farmer's ruined hut and drove for it.

That evening I curled up in one corner of the hut and tried to sleep, while Orestes lay motionless in another corner. My last thought before falling asleep was that if his escape had been prepared, Electra must have known what was going to happen. Tomorrow, crazy or not, Orestes was going to tell me whatever he knew about it.

I awoke to the sound of someone screaming.

I sat up and looked around, disoriented. It felt like the middle of the night, and the light of a quarter moon shone in the ruined window, casting a gentle glow around the room. Orestes was sitting bolt upright. "Why are you after me?" he was shrieking. "Go away!" He waved his arms in the air to bat something away. I looked closely but could see nothing.

I ran over and grabbed his arms. "Orestes! You're dreaming!"

Stronger than he looked, he yanked his arms free. "Don't you see? Look!" He pointed up toward a roof beam, almost invisible in the darkness. "There! Its eyes, dripping with blood. Do you see its teeth? Like a snake's! Oh gods, it's coming back —" his voice broke off with a screech and he batted his arms again, clouting me on the jaw.

I peered around the hut again but could see nothing. I grabbed his shoulders and shook him. "Orestes, there's nothing there. It's just a bad dream."

He looked at me wildly. "I thought so too. But they're not —" his whole body jerked suddenly as though he'd taken a spear thrust. He looked up and screamed. "Get away! Didn't I do what you wanted? Why are you still tormenting me?"

There was no point trying to reason with him, not right now. I darted outside and snatched up the walking stick from the cart. If I couldn't talk him down, there might be another way. "Where are they?" I demanded as I came back in. "Point to them!"

Huddled in the corner, he pointed up toward a rafter.

"There's one. Oh, gods, it's coming down again," he whimpered.

I held the walking stick in both hands and swung it at the empty space he was pointing at. Orestes shrieked, a jubilant tone to his voice. "You hit it. It's backing off!" He looked up and cringed. "Look out — here comes another!" I stepped in front of him and swung the walking stick at the empty air again.

"That's it," he shouted. "You caught its wing. It's gone out the window." He glanced toward the ruined wall. "Here comes the third! She's the worst. The needles, the needles . . . stop her, please stop her!"

I swung the staff hard. He must have imagined I'd scared it off too, because his expression turned to a fierce glee. "She's flown off! Oh, thank you, thank you." He broke off, weeping, and slumped against the wall. Eventually his sobbing died off into snuffles, and ceased altogether.

When I awoke the next morning, he was sitting up.

"Orestes!" He looked up as I approached. "What was that about last night? I want answers now."

He stared silently at me.

"Answer me!" I said loudly. "Or I'll drive off and leave you."

He looked at me, perplexed. "You saw."

I shook my head. "All I saw was you screaming."

"But you fought them."

I sighed. "Orestes, you were imagining them."

He shook his head earnestly. "They're real. The *Erinye*. The Furies. They torment us, the guilty ones. Have you never done anything you've felt guilty about? So guilty that you couldn't eat, couldn't even sleep? That's how they get in."

I started. Did he know about my sister, how I'd hidden while she was captured? No, of course he didn't. He couldn't.

"After the news came of my father's murder," he was saying, "I felt so guilty. If I'd been there, maybe I could have done something." I twitched again. I had almost managed to bury my own guilt, but it came back in a rush as he spoke.

"Then the dreams came," he continued, oblivious to what his words were doing to me. "I thought they were dreams, but they were always the same. They tortured me. Needles under my skin, under my eyelids, screaming at me to avenge my father, keeping me awake . . ." he broke off with a shudder.

I shook off my own guilty reminiscences. At the moment, Orestes sounded — well, not sane, exactly, but willing to talk. If I asked very carefully, I might get answers now. I took a deep breath.

"So you did what they asked?" I prompted him.

He winced. "Yes," he said, his voice hollow.

"So," I asked gently, "how did you do it?"

He clutched at a fold of my chiton. "The Furies told me to. They said it would be all right. He killed my father. He was the king, you know."

I nodded as if this was nothing special. "And how did you do it?" I asked, keeping my tone casual.

He was looking at the far wall, speaking almost to himself. "I came back to Mycenae in disguise. My sister sent a message for me. That night she hid me in my father's bedchamber, to wait for my mother's consort, Aegisthus. When he came to bed I stepped out from behind the tapestry." He looked up at me. "They told me to," he repeated.

It felt like I was pulling a heavy cart with a single horsehair. One tug too hard and I would lose him. "So then . . . what happened?"

He turned his wide blue eyes on me. "He killed my father. He was the king, once. Did you know that? So I had to. I took the knife from my sister. I put it in his chest."

Even though I'd guessed what he was about to say, I stiffened. He'd killed the queen's consort, Aegisthus. No wonder the palace had been in an uproar. "That's that, then," I said, trying to sound reassuring. "You've done what they asked. Your Furies won't come back now." But his next words chilled me anew.

"Oh, I wasn't done," he said calmly. "There was still her."

"Who? Your sister?"

His distant gaze slid off the far wall to fall on me. "Of course not. My mother, she helped. The vengeance wasn't complete yet. So I waited until she came too."

"Deathless gods!" I blurted. "*You killed your own mother?*"

He looked at me, his expression terrifyingly placid, but his hands had begun to tremble. "You do understand, don't you? You said you did. I had to do it."

I tugged my chiton from his grip and stepped back. Killing his mother? Now I knew why he was seeing phantoms. His guilt was eating him up from the inside.

I needed time to think. I stepped out of the farmhouse to draw some water for the donkey and went to fetch some olives and dates for our breakfast. We had food in the cart, but I didn't know how long we would need it to last. Without meaning to, I followed yesterday's cart path back through the grove to the road.

I stopped abruptly as I reached it. The track we had made yesterday was plainly visible, pulling off the road and leaving deep ruts in the soil and long grass between the trees. I felt sweat on my forehead. If the palace guards came down this road after us, as I was now sure they would, they couldn't miss that.

I thought for a moment. They would have spent yesterday searching Mycenae and the road to the port. That could put them on this road today. If they left the palace early in their fast war chariots, they could be here at any moment.

Grabbing a branch, I tried to smooth over the ruts but the soil I was scraping up was wet and dark, making the track stand out even more. I looked up at a sound in the distance. Galloping hooves? I couldn't be sure. Snatching up a handful of the twigs and branches that littered the ground, I ran to sprinkle them across the cart ruts. If I couldn't fill them in, perhaps I could break up the pattern.

The sound was getting louder. I sprinkled some more

leaves across the ruts and scrambled behind a vine-encrusted tree near the road just as a chariot came into sight. I peered out through the vine leaves, my heart racing. A two-horse chariot swept into view carrying a charioteer and a guard in palace armour. Two heavy Mycenaean axes were slung on the front. The guard was peering at the ground on either side, and I held my breath as he passed. Through the vine leaves I could see him glance at the spot where I had half-concealed our tracks, but the chariot rumbled past without stopping, close enough for me to see the foam on the cheek of the near horse.

I waited a few moments before stepping out from behind the tree. Pleased with myself, I had turned and begun to walk back to the hut when a shout came from behind me.

"You! Stop right there!"

I forced myself to turn slowly. A second chariot had come around the bend in the road. Feeling sick about getting caught so easily, I gaped at the two soldiers in it, trying to look like an ignorant peasant. "My lord?"

One of the men looked at me suspiciously as the chariot slowed, rolling to a stop directly in front of the tracks I had half-concealed. "Who are you? What are you doing here? Speak!" he barked.

"Me, my lord?" I said, trying to speak like someone slow of thought. "I'm the son of Aristides, the farmer. He's my father, you see. He's tended these trees since he was younger than me." If I could keep his attention, perhaps he wouldn't look down. "And his father Knoptos before him, and his father

Seligon before him." I scratched my head. "As to what I'm doing here, well, I help my father with the olives," I added. "A grove like this takes a lot of work," I said, gesturing up at the trees around us, "but I'm sure you know that, my lord."

"Yes, yes, I see," said the guard impatiently. "How long have you been here?"

I looked up at the sun through the trees as if gauging the time. "Well, my lord, I've been right here in this patch for perhaps a hand, but here in the grove, I've been since round about sun-up. Now, here on this patch of land, which my father farmed since he was younger than me, I've —"

"Shut up. Have you seen anyone else go by today?"

"Oh yes, sir, certainly."

The guard straightened up. "You have? How long ago?"

"Not long ago at all, sir. In a great hurry, as if they were being chased."

"You did? Which way did they go? Did they turn off anywhere?"

"I wouldn't know that, my lord, as I could only see them on this stretch here. But they didn't turn off while I could see."

"Both? There were two in the cart?"

"There were two of them, bronze and shining just like yours, excepting the dust, of course, which you're likely to pick up riding hard like that. But it was never a cart, sir, it was a chariot."

"A chariot?" the guard shouted. "Idiot! Was there anybody else, not in a chariot?"

"There's no need to be like that, sir, citadel-born though

you be," I said, trying to sound reproachful. "I'm trying to answer, and it's not my fault if you ask the wrong questions." I added, as if by afterthought, "Still, I haven't seen anyone other than the two I spoke of, for the chariot had a driver and —"

"Be still, you fool." The guard turned back to his charioteer. "Drive on. This simpleton can't help us."

The charioteer snapped the reins and they rolled away. I stood still, gaping after them in case they turned back to look, and breathed a careful sigh of relief as they vanished around the bend. This time I waited until I was sure there were no others before hiding our cart tracks more carefully and returning to the farmer's hut.

That night I was awakened again by Orestes' screams. His eyes were wide open and he was sitting up in the moonlight, raising his arms as if protecting himself. Great. There wasn't much point telling him that he was dreaming. I picked up the walking stick again. If I could convince him I had chased them off, we might get some sleep.

As I swung it toward the mouldering rafters, I thought of our conversation that morning, and a guilty recollection wormed its way into my mind. Here I was, defending Orestes from imaginary creatures. Why hadn't I defended my sister Melantha from the Greeks, the night they had taken her? I could have done something. Instead I'd cowered beneath a blanket while the Greeks took my sister away.

A sharp pang of guilt jabbed at me, draining me of strength.

As I struggled to swing the walking stick again, something seemed to move among the roof beams. Peering into the darkness, I could almost make out a shape clinging to the rafters, staring at Orestes behind me. I blinked, but the form was still there, wraith-like, shadowy talons clutching at crossbeams in the ceiling.

A head turned as if sensing my gaze, and I froze. Was I seeing this, or was it a trick of the moonlight? For an instant there had been a hag's face in the darkness, its bloodless lips drawn back and distorted, nostrils flared as if scenting a meal. The thing, if it was there, seemed to gesture, a phantom arm twitching in my direction. As another wave of guilt pressed down on me, making me stagger, its gaze snapped back toward me and its eyes locked onto mine.

This time the guilt struck like a giant's club, knocking me to my knees. I sensed wings unfold above me in the gloom, and felt something swoop down. I was fighting to stand but the overwhelming guilt and shame were sucking the life from my body.

Invisible talons clasped my skull. The pain was intense, as if needles were driving deep into my head. A half-formed face floated before me.

"You could have saved her, couldn't you?" a voice hissed from deep inside my head. "You let her die, at the hands of those animals, those *Greeks.*"

How did it know? "No!" I repeated desperately, guilt stifling me. "I didn't . . . she's alive . . ."

The scabby face came closer, drawing a long breath through

its nose, eyes closed in horrible rapture. "You think that's better?" the voice in my head whispered. "What torment is she going through now? Perhaps even this instant. And you could have saved her from it all. But you were a coward, weren't you?" The face bent and sniffed deeply at me again.

How could it know these things? The wraith was digging my innermost fears from me, plucking them out like eyes, drowning me in a pool of my own shame. It was true. I could have saved her. If only I hadn't been such a coward. I didn't deserve to live.

The pressure of guilt redoubled, making me retch, worthless worm that I was. As I closed my eyes, I was dimly aware of two other creatures like the first, flitting and gibbering in the background, ecstatically breathing the fumes of my shame, draining my soul. I deserved to die, slowly and painfully —

There was a sound of bronze, and the needles piercing my skull were suddenly gone. I opened my eyes. Before me stood Orestes, thrusting at something with his unsheathed sword.

I shook my head as if awakening from a nightmare. What had I been thinking? I didn't know if these things were real, but I stepped forward and swung the walking stick anyway. The staff moved like a blade through water, slicing through one of the shapes as if it wasn't there. It lifted its hideous face and turned back to me.

Bracing myself against the buzzing guilt, I swung the staff again, watching the wood pass through it as if through a curtain of smoke. A voice in my head screeched, and something retreated to the ceiling and vanished. A second shape eluded Orestes to dive on me but as my staff sliced through what might have been a wing, or a trick of the moonlight, the creature made an unearthly noise in my head and vanished through the ruined roof. I spun around to face the third creature, but its smoky wings flapped, and the shape darted out after the others.

Orestes and I stared at one another in the faint glow of approaching dawn. His vacant stare was gone, his eyes aflame. "Are you all right?"

I nodded. "Were those . . . real?"

He shrugged. "They're real to me."

After tonight, I would never dismiss anyone who claimed to see things I couldn't. "Why are they after you?"

Orestes looked uncomfortable. "I think they feed on . . . guilt. Why they went for you, I don't know."

I did. I had let the Greeks take my sister. No wonder my guilt had revealed me to them.

He glanced down at his sword. "I could never fight them before. All that guilt, it was paralyzing. But when they attacked you, it was different. I couldn't let it happen to someone else."

Over a dinner that evening of olives, dates and cheese, I began to learn more about him. He was the son of King Agamemnon and Queen Clytamnestra, the former king and queen of Mycenae, as he'd said earlier. When he was twelve, his father had set off to war with Troy. Soon afterwards, his mother had sent him out of town, before inviting Orestes' uncle Aegisthus into the palace to live with her.

"Electra told me that our mother was careful never to call Aegisthus a king, though," he said, spitting out an olive pit. "Just her consort. It made her look more legitimate. She needed a prop, not a king."

I nodded. "Why did your — I mean, why were you sent away?"

He frowned. "So Aegisthus couldn't kill me. But I didn't understand that then. It hurt."

Palace intrigue wasn't something I'd ever followed, back in Troy. "Why? I mean, why would he kill you?"

He sighed. "I'm the heir to the throne, Alexi," he said patiently. "If Aegisthus killed me, his own son could become king. My mother . . . she would have known that." His hands trembled.

I nodded. "What made you come back?"

"I'd been sent to my uncle, King Strophios. He's got a small kingdom on Mount Parnassus, south of Delphi. Near the Delphic Oracle. I didn't like my uncle much, but I got along with his son Pylades. I spent twelve years there. Three years ago, I was kicking around, starting to wonder what to do with my life, when word came that my father had died, just after coming home from the Trojan War.

"I was about to return to Mycenae to take the kingship, but my uncle told me Aegisthus would kill me the moment I walked in. With what I know now, I'm sure he was right."

He hesitated. "I was asleep one night when those *things* appeared. I thought it was a dream. They began tormenting me, screaming that I was a disgrace to my lineage, that I had failed to honour my father. It was crushing me." He shook his head.

"They said they would stop if I avenged my father. I didn't know what they were talking about. We'd heard that father had died in his sleep. But the *Erinye* kept after me.

"One day a man came to the palace from Mycenae with a private message for me from my sister Electra. The message was 'Come back. He was murdered.'"

Orestes turned to look at me. "You know the strangest thing? I was relieved. I'd felt so guilty, but I'd never understood why. When I got that message, I realized that I'd never really believed my father had died in his sleep. So I came back, pretending to be my cousin Pylades. That got me into the palace, and Electra told me what had really happened." He shuddered, looking at his feet.

"Electra saw it. It was the day he got back from Troy." He hesitated. "My mother had the slaves draw him a hot bath. As soon as he got in, she and Aegisthus held him down under the water."

He raised his head to look at me. "But he was a strong man, and he almost got free. So Aegisthus stood on his chest. My mother came back in with an axe. They butchered my father like an animal. His head was almost cut from his body! That's why I had to . . . do what I did. It was the way to stop my guilt. Those *things*." He fell silent, staring at his hands, which were trembling violently once more.

"So, this Delphic oracle," I said quickly. "What's that?"

He looked up, distracted. "You don't know? I thought you were Greek."

"Of course I am," I began, struggling for an answer. "But I, uh, grew up in the country, though, so I've only heard of it."

He looked at me. "Not it. *Her*. The Pythia's a woman. The god Apollo speaks directly through her. It's because of the location."

I nodded.

"You have no idea, do you?" Orestes said, watching my expression closely. "You really are from the country. Delphi is the very centre of the world, the *omphalos*. The navel. That's why she's the most powerful oracle in the world. Whatever your question is, she knows the answer."

"You said it wasn't far from your uncle's kingdom. Do you know how to get there?"

He frowned. "I guess so. Why?"

It felt like a fire was creeping outwards from my chest. This oracle could tell me how to find my sister. "Because I need to go there," I said firmly. "And you're coming with me."

CHAPTER SIX

The Oracle's Message

"THERE'S NO ROOM HERE. Go away." The inn's wooden door had a small, face-sized portal set into it, which the innkeeper slammed shut as he spoke. I was about to move on, but Orestes spoke up. "But we have trade goods. Gems." He tugged a small leather purse from inside his travelling cloak and pulled out a rounded cabochon ruby as big as my little fingernail. "Look."

The portal snapped open. "Gems?"

Orestes held the ruby up. The innkeeper's surly expression cracked for a moment. "I suppose you can stay the night," he grumbled. Orestes nodded.

"That's one ruby apiece, of course," the innkeeper added quickly. "Per night. And the donkey stays out."

I turned to Orestes. "This inn doesn't look like much," I said loudly.

He looked puzzled for a moment, but caught on quickly. "You're right," he replied. "Let's find something that suits a king's son better. And doesn't cost so much. This is Corinth, not Mycenae."

Another bolt slid across, and the innkeeper swung the entire door open. He was a heavyset man with a dishevelled, greying beard and a large bald patch on top of his head. "No, no," he said, bowing low. "A king's son? I've got the finest rooms. Ask anyone." His voice had that greasy, wheedling tone that I'd heard unpleasant people use when they were trying to be friendly. "And for a king's son, with gems, I'm sure we can work out a deal." He rubbed his hands and beckoned to someone behind him. "Samanthos. Come here!"

He turned back to us. "Cursed slaves. Always slouching off when you need them. *Samanthos!*" A small boy appeared behind him. "Take these gentlemen's donkey and cart around to the stable. Get it some water and hay."

I looked over at Orestes with the tiniest of nods. He stepped back and looked down the street as if measuring the effort of finding another inn, then nodded reluctantly. "We'll bring our goods to our room with us," he said firmly. The innkeeper's face fell, and I realized he'd been looking forward to searching our bundles. We unloaded the cart and the innkeeper showed us upstairs to a room whose stone walls were hung with tapestries that had once been colourful but were now completely faded. One of the door's bronze hinge posts had snapped off and been replaced with a leather strap. There was no bolt on the door.

I turned to Orestes after the innkeeper had clumped back down the steps. "Those rubies — do you know how valuable they are?" I'd heard the Greeks talk about them, back when I'd been a slave. "One of those could keep us here for a month."

Orestes shrugged. "Of course it could. But if the hope of more rubies keeps him on our side, it's worth it."

I glanced at him in surprise. Since we'd left the farmhouse ten days ago, he'd opened up, becoming more reliable, even likeable. I was glad I hadn't dumped him that first night on the road.

That evening, the innkeeper brought us a greasy meal of roast goat wrapped in grape leaves and a pitcher of water with two goblets. "Is there anything else I can do for you?" he asked. Even his voice sounded oily.

I waved him away impatiently, but Orestes called him back. "How far are we from Delphi?" he asked.

The innkeeper turned back to us. "So it's Delphi you're heading for, is it?" he said, rubbing his hands.

"Perhaps," I said warily. With just the two of us travelling, and a bag of gems, I didn't want anyone knowing our business.

"The Pythia, she's helped a lot of people," the innkeeper volunteered. "Kings and such. You're looking for advice from the priestess, are you? Have you brought treasure?"

I spoke up before Orestes could answer. "Our business with the Pythia is private."

He looked wounded. "Just trying to help, good sirs, that's all." He turned to Orestes. "The way's not so long, perhaps twenty days overland. But it's not so safe as it used to be, what with the bandits and all. Fifteen years ago, the local lords used to sweep the roads clear." His tone turned strangely wistful. "But since the war, that's all fallen off. More than your life's worth to travel overland to Delphi now."

He paused at the door. "Just so you know, sirs, my brother-in-law is a fisherman. His boat could take you straight across the gulf of Korinthos and drop you at the very foot of the mountain. It'd be just a quick trip on foot beyond that."

That sounded better. The next morning the innkeeper took us to his brother-in-law. We found him sitting on a stone breakwater on the beach, mending his nets. He was completely bald, his black beard trimmed short.

"We need a boat to take us to Delphi," I explained. "Can you take us in yours?"

He finished cutting out a frayed strand in his net before answering. "Aye."

I waited for him to add something. "Well, um, that's good," I said at last. Fighting the impulse to fill in the silence, I added, "Do you . . . is there anything you want to ask us?"

He knotted a new strand into place. "Nay." He spat on the ground. "Dawn tomorrow."

Orestes stepped forward. "About payment, Captain . . ."

He nodded toward the innkeeper. "Talk to him." He began running a new stretch of net through his fingers, searching for rips.

I nodded. "Goodbye, then." He ignored us.

As we walked back up the street to the inn, the innkeeper rubbed his hands together anxiously. "Don't mind him," he said. "That's just his way. Never said much, even as a boy. But he's a good sailor. Now," he continued, his voice turning even oilier, "as to payment, you've got some rubies . . ."

We settled on a single cabochon ruby from Orestes' bag to cover our passage, and grossly overpaid the innkeeper with a second ruby, for which he swore he would look after our cart and donkey until we returned, as if they were his own children.

We arrived the next morning just as the sun was coming over the horizon. His boat was already waiting in the water, two greying but muscular rowers on each side and the captain on the steering oar. We climbed aboard with our travelling sacks, my nose wrinkling at the overpowering scent of fish. The rowers put up the sail and took us out of the harbour. With the sail catching a stiff wind, we made good time for most of the morning. If things continued this way it would be a quick crossing.

It was around mid-morning when the men, at a grunt

from the captain, took the sail down. The wind was still a good one, and I watched with concern as the captain let go of his steering oar and came forward to the bow deck, where Orestes and I were sitting.

"What's the matter?" I asked.

"Need another one," he grunted.

I didn't like the sound of that. "Another what?"

"One o' them." He pointed to the bag Orestes kept his stash of rubies in. "Or we go back."

"What?" I demanded. "We paid you already!"

The captain shrugged.

Orestes grabbed my arm. "What do we do now?" he whispered anxiously. "I knew this was a bad idea, going to Delphi."

I tugged my arm free. "Can we talk privately for a moment, Captain?" I asked, trying to sound calm. "We have to decide if we can afford it."

The captain frowned. "Be quick." We walked over to the far side of the foredeck and leaned over the rail.

"I've heard of this," Orestes said. "They get the traveller out in the boat and change the deal. We have to do what they say or they'll slit our throats!"

I thought for a moment. "How many rubies do you have?"

He peeked in the bag. "About twenty, I think. But we'll need them for the oracle, won't we?"

I nodded. "I have an idea. Give me the biggest one. Hold the bag over the railing."

Orestes looked at me uncertainly but reached into his bag

and handed over the largest gem I'd ever seen, a smooth, rounded ruby the size of my little toe. I stepped away from the rail, holding the ruby above my head. The captain moved to intercept me but I dodged around him.

"Sailors!" I cried over the flapping of the furled sail. "I want to offer you a reward!"

The men's eyes widened as I held up the ruby. "I will give this gem to the sailor who deserves it most, the instant we reach the coast at Delphi." Behind me, the captain let out an angry growl.

"I'm certain you're all honest men," I went on, "but just the same, if anyone tries to step onto the forward deck, I will immediately give this ruby to the man who throws him overboard. And if you all approach us together, I will throw this ruby overboard, and anything else I have of value. Step back, Captain."

The captain took an angry step toward me but Orestes stretched his hand over the rail, dangling the bag of gemstones over the water. The men began to clamour and the captain backed off, snarling.

"That was brilliant!" Orestes said, his eyes shining, as I rejoined him at the bow rail. "Do you think it will work?"

I nodded toward the sailors. "Look at them. They're just waiting for someone to move so they can dump him overboard. But the captain's furious. And I'm not sure what to do when we land. That's when they'll rush us."

"Do you have any ideas?" Orestes asked anxiously.

I shrugged. "Perhaps. How good are you with a sword?"

"A sword?" He sounded uncertain. "Not too bad. My uncle, King Strophios, made me train with his son Pylades. But if you think I can take on four sailors, plus the captain —"

"No, of course not," I interrupted. "Here's what I want you to do. When we beach, take your sack and run up the beach a bit. Keep your sword out. Stay close enough that you can hear me, but far enough to have a good head start if they chase you. Leave the rest up to me."

It was early afternoon when there was a shout from one of the sailors, and I turned to see a shoreline in the distance. As we drew closer, I could see a small fishing village. The sailors brought the sail down and rowed the ship in, bringing the bow up onto the beach just below the village. I stood up in the bow, holding the ruby in one hand, my travelling staff in the other. With the men's attention focused on me, Orestes grabbed his travelling sack and leapt over the prow.

As he stopped a short distance away, I spoke, trying to give my voice the confidence of Lopex. "You have all performed your duties admirably," I said loudly. "It's hard to say who deserves this most."

"Take him now!" the captain burst out.

I held up the ruby so they could all see it, and tossed it into the bottom of the boat, where it rolled and buried itself under a pile of fishing nets. As the sailors jumped for it, I vaulted over the bow rail and ran to join Orestes. The captain was shouting at the men to go after us, but they ignored him, groping beneath the net. As I caught up with Orestes, panting, one of the sailors gave a triumphant cry.

I turned to see him holding up the ruby. The delight in his face turned to dismay as the other sailors advanced on him, reaching for their knives. "Let's go," I said grimly. "They'll be busy for a while." We turned and set off up the path toward Delphi.

The path up the mountain led almost immediately into woods and a mist so thick I could hardly see my feet. As we ascended, I was startled more than once when the fog cleared momentarily to reveal a sheer cliff to my left.

Orestes seemed not to notice. Since we'd left the farmhouse he had become more talkative, as if a weight had been lifted from him. "That was clever, back in the boat," he said, as we followed a loamy stretch of path wide enough for us to walk side by side. "I never would have thought of that."

"It wasn't all my idea," I admitted, embarrassed. "I'd heard something like it, once before."

Orestes looked interested, so I went on, remembering the story I'd heard one night at the slaves' fire. "There was a very pretty Greek princess, years ago," I said. "She had a lot of suitors. Her father was afraid to choose one for her, afraid that the other suitors would kill him."

Orestes was looking at me strangely. "Go on," he said.

"Her father made them all swear an oath to defend whoever he gave her to. So even if one of the other suitors got angry and tried to kill him — the man she was given to, I mean — the rest of them would have to stop him.

"I didn't think an oath would work here, but that's where I got the idea. The sailors kept each other honest."

Orestes didn't say anything for a little while. "You do know that story is about my Aunt Helen, don't you?" he said, as we picked our way up a rocky slope.

"Sure," I said. "Paris's bride, Helen. Wait — she was your aunt?"

He nodded. "My mother" — he flinched at the word but recovered quickly — "was her sister. But her father might as well have saved himself the effort. Aunt Helen ran off with some Trojan prince a few years later. The war started when the Trojans wouldn't give her back." His face contorted. "A lot of my friends never came back from that war. At least Troy was destroyed," he added grimly. I held my tongue.

Since it was too late to reach Delphi that day, we stopped as evening fell in a rotting wooden shack built to shelter a small shrine to Hermes. I figured that as the patron god of travellers, he would understand. Orestes carefully laid his travelling cloak in the darkest corner, farthest from the entrance.

"Are they still after you?" I asked. "After all, you, um, did what they wanted."

He didn't answer for a moment, and I was afraid I'd sent him into one of his moods again. After a little while, he spoke. "At first, it was for what I didn't do," he said quietly. "I didn't avenge my father. Then, I think it was for what I did. I avenged my father, but to do it I killed . . . I killed my mother."

"That's not fair," I burst out. "They told you to!"

He shook his head. "I don't understand it. But since the farmhouse, I know they will never leave me alone."

I nodded in sympathy, but part of me wasn't surprised. In the stories my grandmother used to tell me of the Greek gods, they could be angry, fickle, jealous, or even crazy, but never fair.

It was around noon the next day that the road left the forest behind and crossed a broad plain. On a hillside at the far end was a temple, surrounded by a cluster of buildings. We had reached Delphi.

"I don't know," Orestes said. "Are we in the right place?"

After a dusty climb up the hillside, we found ourselves standing before a large temple to Apollo, god of prophecies. It towered over us, a painted marble statue of Apollo looking down from the roof with flashing eyes, but it looked untended, coated with dust and graffiti scratchings. I couldn't read the words, but I recognized a large letter epsilon on one of the pillars, as if someone had started to write something before deciding it wasn't worth it. Except for a couple of stray dogs panting in the shade and a half-dozen clucking chickens, the dusty street was deserted.

"I thought it would be a little grander," said Orestes, sounding disappointed.

I glanced over at him and he shrugged apologetically. "All my life, I've heard about Delphi. Centre of the world. Seat of the mighty Oracle. And look at this." He gestured at the deserted town. As if on cue, a crow squawked from atop Apollo's head.

We approached the temple cautiously. "Hello?" I called. "Is there anyone here?"

A discoloured flap of sailcloth hanging between two pillars flipped aside and a man emerged. He was wearing a priest's blue chiton, stained with wine in several places. "What?" he grumbled.

Orestes seemed dismayed, but a grumpy, wine-stained priest seemed about right for the place. I nudged Orestes, who found his voice again and spoke in the formal Greek style used on such occasions.

"I greet you, O priest," he said. "I am Orestes, son of Agamemnon, late king of Mycenae. My mother, Queen Clytamnestra, sends her greetings. We beg through you the assistance of the god Apollo."

The priest scratched his greasy hair. "King of Mycenae, eh? So what did you bring?"

Orestes blinked. "Pardon me, O priest?"

The priest frowned impatiently. "Your offering, boy. You want help from the god, it's not free. What did you bring? Not more goats, I hope. Hades, I'm getting so tired of goat meat. Some suckling pig, now, that would be nice."

Caught off guard, Orestes stammered for a moment before

recovering and bringing out two rubies from his sack. "We, uh, offer these two rubies in return for the help of the god."

The priest hardly glanced at them. "Can't eat rubies, boy. What else have you got?"

"What else?" I blurted. "These are cabochon rubies. Any one of these is worth . . ." I hesitated, trying to imagine what a ruby might be worth. "A new marble statue in the temple. Or maybe two."

The priest turned his gaze on me. "So give it to a sculptor, boy. It's no good here."

Orestes frowned, looking almost princely for a moment. "Is this the way of the priests at Delphi? You reject gifts of glory to your god to fill your belly?"

The priest turned to look at Orestes. "Look, Son. Things have changed," he said, sounding tired. "Back twenty years, we had visitors. Kings and princes, nobility and commoners. All here for the word of the god. Herds of pure white bulls. They took days to sacrifice. *Days.*" The fatigue seemed to fall from his face as he remembered.

"But something happened. The crowds thinned. Then they stopped. Nowadays, we get only a few visitors a month. They say the overland route is too dangerous, so they come by sea. And even that has its problems."

I couldn't help myself. "What changed?"

The priest turned to me with a shrug. "I wouldn't know, kid," he said. "We don't get much news here. But from what I've heard, there was a war. Off to the east somewhere. In

Troad, I think. Kings and commoners, they all went off. Not many came back. And Delphi, centre of the world, was forgotten. My acolytes drifted away, until there was just me. And the Pythia, of course. I hope the war was worth it, because it took our soul."

He seemed to catch himself and turned back to Orestes. "So don't be too quick to condemn, young man. I could have forsaken my oath and abandoned the Pythia, but I stayed. And if nowadays my focus is as much on my dinner as my duty, I am still here."

I had a sudden thought. "How about this?" I asked, bringing out the jewelled gold bracelet that Electra had given me.

"What's that?" Orestes said, grabbing my wrist. "That's my sister's!"

I nodded. "She gave it to me to buy passage on a ship, the night I left Mycenae. I think she was hoping to frame me for stealing it."

Orestes looked embarrassed. "Sorry about that. She's always been a schemer. I'm glad that one didn't work out." He turned to the priest and held the bracelet up. "Well? How about this?"

The priest shook his head. "Sorry, Son. Got no use for jewellery either. If you've got no animals to sacrifice, we've got nothing to talk about. Too bad. Sounds like you've got some interesting stories." He turned and headed back to the temple.

I turned to Orestes. "You said the oracle was a woman?" I

said, looking at the bracelet. "I have an idea. Keep him distracted." I snatched the bracelet back and darted off around the corner of the temple.

The temple had pillars around the front and sides, and I ducked in between the side pillars. At the back of the temple, where a statue of the temple's god would usually stand, was a small room with walls of cut stone. I slipped in through a leather flap set into one wall.

In the centre of the dim room was an uneven crevice in the floor, over which a wooden bench hung by two ropes from the ceiling, like a swing. In the corner, on a stool, crouched a young woman, a few years older than me, wearing a simple white robe. Her black hair had been cut almost to her scalp, and her skin was as white as bone, as though the sun had never touched it. "Are you the Pythia?" I asked.

She looked up at me. "You shouldn't be here," she said calmly. "Theoclymenos wouldn't like it."

I squatted down against the wall nearby. "My lady," I began uncertainly, holding out the bracelet on my palm, "may I offer you this?"

She looked at it curiously. "What does it do?"

I paused. Now that I thought about it, I wasn't sure why girls liked jewellery. "It — it makes you pretty." Oops. "Prettier, I mean."

She reached out a hand for it.

"Allow me," I said. "You wear it like this." I slipped it onto her thin wrist and brought over the oil lamp. She held up her arm and gasped as the jewels sparkled in the lamp light. "Is this for me?"

"If you'd like it."

She took her eyes from it. "You want to find something. It troubles you," she said. "I can feel it hissing in you, like steam." She reached out to touch my shoulder but jerked her hand back in surprise.

I jumped to my feet. "What is it?" I asked.

She turned her face slowly upward to me, wonder in her expression. "I can't help you."

"What?" I said, startled.

"You have already been marked by the god," she said. "You have an answer from a prophet far more powerful than I. It would be an insult to ask again. I'm sorry." She slipped the bracelet off. "I'm sorry to give this back," she said. "I cannot take payment without service."

I hadn't realized how much I'd been counting on her answer. I felt crushed.

"I sense your distress," she said. "I wish I could help you."

"It's too bad you can't do something for my companion," I said, trying to contain my disappointment. "But he doesn't need a prophesy. His problems are all inside."

"Is he ill?"

I shook my head. "Inside his head, I mean. At least, I think so," I added, remembering the half-shapes I'd glimpsed in the moonlight. "He calls them the *Erinye*."

She gasped. "*Erinye*? Your friend is beset by the Furies?"

"Or his imagination. But it made him do something terrible." I explained.

The Pythia looked at me strangely. "But that would never work! The *Erinye* persecute wrongs within a family. Especially children who wrong their parents." She paused. "Did he really . . . do that?"

I nodded. "To avenge his father, killed by his own wife."

She closed her eyes as if to shut out the image. "So much pain, for one family. Mother against father, son against mother . . . tell me, has it worked? Have the *Erinye* left him alone?"

I shook my head.

"It is not his imagination, then. The *Erinye* will pursue him until he dies. They say it's the smell of sin that draws them." Her eyes opened suddenly. "Perhaps I can help your friend after all. Please bring him to me." She held up her wrist with the bracelet and gave a shy smile. "I'm glad. I really like this."

The next day, as we trekked back down the path through the trees lining the mountain flanks, neither of us said much. I was preoccupied with what the Oracle had told me, and whatever she had said or done to Orestes had left him just as silent.

Eventually, as we set off again after lunch, he spoke.

"I have to go back to Mycenae."

I glanced at him, startled. After all the effort his sister had put into getting him out, that was the last thing I'd expected him to say.

He nodded. "It sounds stupid. But the oracle helped me. She . . . purified me."

I ducked under another hanging branch. The road to Delphi had been well maintained once, but was now crumbling and overgrown. "Go on."

"It was weird. She said the *Erinye* could smell my sin. That's how they found me. She poured some pig's blood on my head, then wiped me down with an olive bough. She said it would cleanse me of my blood guilt. For killing my mother."

It was the first time I'd seen him say that without flinching. "Yes," he said, as if reading my thoughts. "I can talk about it now. The oracle also told me the *Erinye* are older than man, maybe even than the gods. They don't care about fairness, only retribution. But thanks to her, they aren't after me anymore!" He grabbed my arm. "Alexi, I can reclaim my kingship!"

I stared at him.

"Also, she said it's my destiny." He sounded almost embarrassed. "So what did she tell you?"

It took me a moment to adjust. When I first met him, Orestes couldn't even speak. Now he was planning to go back and retake his father's throne. With an effort, I switched mental horses and repeated what the oracle had said to me.

"She said you've already been told?" he asked curiously. "So you've been to an oracle before, then?"

I shook my head. "Never. I don't know what she meant."

"You're sure? They say people sometimes misunderstand her."

I used my walking stick to vault over a damp patch trickling across the path. "Those were her exact words. But I've never been to an oracle. The closest was crazy Cass, a slave girl in Mycenae. But she was wrong. She always is," I added. "Everyone knows that."

Orestes, with his longer legs, stepped over the damp spot and came up beside me. "How do you know?" he asked. "What did she say?"

I thought back. "Something about rowing. Someone who rows to the fore, and how he would find her. It didn't make any sense. Like I said, she's crazy."

"Are you sure?" Orestes asked, glancing at me. "If that's the only oracular-type prediction you've ever had, it must be what the Pythia meant."

I shrugged. "Look, I told you already, Cass is crazy. Nobody believes her." I thought of something else. "She said something about 'the son she sent away, who returns as a viper to take vengeance.' What's that about? I don't know what —" I ran into Orestes as he stopped dead in front of me on the trail.

"*She said that?*" he asked, grabbing me by both shoulders.

"Uh, yes," I said. "Why?"

"When?" he demanded.

I shrugged. "Perhaps a half month before I left Mycenae," I said. "Why? Like I said, she's crazy."

His grip on my shoulders was almost painful. "You really don't see it, do you? 'The son she sent away.' Who do you think she was talking about? My mother sent me away when my father went to war. And 'returns to take vengeance.' When your slave girl said that I was only a few days away from Mycenae, coming back to avenge my father." He shook his head. "This is incredible. Alexi, how could you not notice? What else did she say?"

I looked over at him, irritated. "Orestes, she's crazy. Everyone knows that."

Orestes looked at me closely. "Something's going on. You're too smart for this. Even with proof, you don't believe her." He peered into my eyes. "It's like you're under a curse. So listen closely, Alexi. If she told you to look for someone who rows to the fore, do it."

We reached the fishing village that evening. A coastal trading ship had put in that afternoon to trade goods and refill their cisterns. The next morning we found the captain loading the last of a cargo of sponges. Orestes put a cautionary hand on my arm. "Let's see if we can work our passage. Buying our way didn't work too well."

I nodded. "Captain!" I called out.

He glanced at us, a lean man with a face like cracked red leather. "Yes?"

"I am Alexias of Heraklion, and this is Orestes of Mycenae. Where are you bound?"

The captain kept his eyes on the men loading nets of dried sponges. "Korinthos this evening, then west toward the cape.

We follow the coast. Why?"

"We'd like to work passage on your ship to Korinthos."

The captain's eye flickered over us. "I'll take you," he said, pointing to Orestes. "We're short-handed on rowers. Not you," he added, glancing at me. "You're too short."

I felt a surge of anger. "But I'm a sailor!" Or close enough. As the captain of the *Sappho* had pointed out, I knew my way around a rope.

He guffawed. "Kid, if I had a sheepskin for everyone who tried to talk their way on board with that line . . . well, I'd have a lot of sheepskin," he finished lamely.

I walked over to inspect the ship. It was narrower and shorter than the cargo-carrying *Sappho* that had brought me to Mycenae, with seven rowing benches stretched across an open hold, and small decks at the bow and stern. Before the wind it would be faster than the *Sappho* too, but nowhere near the speed of the *Pelagios*.

It was also badly maintained. Many of the ropes were frayed and had been spliced over and over. Half of the oar lock posts looked broken or loose, and the mast, which they had left up, had snapped at some point. Instead of replacing it, the crew had clumsily lashed the two halves back together.

"Suit yourself, Captain," I said, shrugging. "But your port backstay isn't tied off properly. Sail like that and the first good gust will pull it free. You might even lose the mast. Again."

The captain glanced in the direction I had pointed. "Don't be silly," he began, but looked again at the rope. "Deiophon!"

he shouted. "What are you playing at? Re-tie that port back-stay before we sail!"

He glanced back at me thoughtfully. "Fine, then," he said. "Get on. Maybe you'll be some use." We scrambled to help push the ship into the water, and boarded with the rest of the crew.

The wind was with us on the way back, and the captain kept me busy adjusting the sail. When we tied up at the Korinthos wharf late that afternoon, the captain began bartering with some merchants near the pier, and Orestes collected his travelling sack. "Our friend the innkeeper had better have kept our cart safe," he said, turning to me. "What are you going to do?"

"I'm not sure," I admitted. "The captain tells me he trades his way around the coast. He's willing to let me sail with him." I shrugged. "I guess it sounds kind of stupid, searching all of the Greek lands for my sister."

Orestes shook his head. "I think that's a mistake. Looking for your sister is fine, but you need a plan or you'll spend your whole life at it. The men who took your sister probably sold her. Do you know anything else about them? It could cut down your search a lot."

He still thought they were rogue slave traders, kidnapping a girl from a Greek village. "Orestes, there's something I haven't told you," I said, taking a deep breath. "My sister wasn't Greek. She was taken from Troy by Greek warriors, the night that Troy fell."

Orestes stared at me. "From Troy? What was she doing there?"

I waited for him to figure it out.

He stared at me. "Your sister was Trojan? But that means . . . you must be Trojan too," he said slowly. I nodded.

His perplexed look shifted, becoming a frown, then angry. "Trojan!" he repeated, his jaw tightening. "So you've been lying about that all this time?"

I spread my hands in a half shrug and said nothing, hoping to ride out his anger.

"Do you know how many friends of mine died in that war, Trojan?" he snapped. "How many Greeks?" I shook my head.

"I'm sorry I ever trusted you. Just thank your gods I'm not turning you in. The king of Korinthos can always use more Trojan slaves." He climbed over the bow rail onto the dock and walked away stiffly.

"Orestes!" I called to him. "I've been honest about everything else. I just couldn't tell anyone about . . . that." I stopped, shocked. Kassander had said the same thing to me once. And I'd reacted exactly as Orestes just did.

He kept walking. "Orestes!" I called again. "I didn't believe you about the Furies, but I fought them anyway!"

He took another few steps and stopped. "You did," he said, turning slowly. "Twice." He seemed to think it over. "I guess it doesn't suit the future king of Mycenae to turn his back on a friend like that, does it?"

He came back along the pier and held out a hand. "Come

on down. Let's get our cart. If it was soldiers who took her, she's probably a slave in one of the citadels. Don't waste your time with fishing villages."

I picked up my travelling sack and climbed over the rail onto the pier. "Why?"

"After a war, the kings get the slaves, especially the pretty ones. You've been to Mycenae already. You should go to Sparta. My aunt Helen lives there with my Uncle Menelaus. Tell her you bring greetings from me and I'm sure you'll be welcome. She can help you find your sister, if she's there."

I nodded. "Thanks."

"I'll drop you at Tiryns. It's on the way to Argos, where I'm going to find the nobles still loyal to my father. I'm sure you can talk your way onto a ship bound for Sparta from there."

CHAPTER SEVEN

Helen of Sparta

ORESTES PRESSED A SMALL bag of rubies into my hand and gave me a powerful hug as we reached the docks at Tiryns. "I'd give you more if I could," he said apologetically, "but I'm going to need them for my fight. You'll always be welcome at the palace of Mycenae, once it's mine again. Even if you are Trojan." He winked, climbed into the cart and rode off.

Four of the six ships at the jetty weren't bound for Sparta, and of the two that were, one didn't plan to leave for a month. The captain of the last ship, a coastal trader, looked at me quizzically when I told him I was a sailor looking for a berth as far as Sparta, but took me on board without argument.

I spent the next six months on the *Arethusa* as she crept along the coast of what Captain Alcimedon called Peloponneseus, the island of Pelops. "She's not really an island at all," he remarked to me one day. "She's connected to the mainland by a land channel at Korinthos. But she's got the name now, and most likely will for eternity."

In spite of Orestes' advice, I couldn't help asking after my sister at every port, but he was right. Most of them were small fishing villages, too small and poor for slaves. In the few towns with a great house, none of the in-town merchants had seen a grey-eyed slave girl with straight black hair, although several, with a wink and a nod, were sure they could find me one.

"Keep a sharp lookout for raiders," Captain Alcimedon was fond of saying when we were at sea. "They'll be doing us the same favour." I'd been started as ship's boy but when he'd discovered one day that I had better eyesight than his lookout, I was switched into the stern to watch for raiders.

"They come up from behind, most times," the captain told me. "They have fast ships, a lot of rowers, but they don't carry much water." He grabbed my arm sharply as I went to rest against the stern rail. "Don't lean on that. Where was I? Oh. An empty cistern makes them light and fast in the chase, but they can't keep it up. If you can avoid them for a hand or two, they'll give up. So the more warning you can give us, the more chance we have to open a gap. If we're quick enough, sometimes they don't give chase at all."

When I asked the captain how he knew so much about

raider tactics, he shot a glance at me. "Don't get smart, boy. I've never crewed a raider. But you don't trade this coast for twenty years without learning a lot about them. They've gotten worse since the war ended."

Their preferred tactic, I learned, was to hide in a cove and come out at high speed as a likely ship passed. "Why don't they attack from ahead?" I asked.

"They will, if they can," the captain said grimly. "But only if they can see us coming and have the wind of their target." He shuddered. "That's the worst. You're rowing direct into the wind, and suddenly they're dead ahead. Now you've got to turn the ship and get the sail up. By the time you're done, they've closed right up with you, running under sail and pulling oars at the same time." He looked at me. "Ever pull a bow, Son?"

I shook my head.

"Time you learned. If we've ever got raiders close on our wake, I need archers in the stern, and I can't spare rowers."

That evening, after we'd landed and made camp for the night, he came by with a bow and some arrows. After some practice, my accuracy hadn't improved, but it turned out I had a strong draw. "That's fine," the captain said. "We're not shooting the eye out of a sparrow. The farther you can shoot, the farther away you can drop an arrow on their deck."

It was less than a month later that I learned what he was talking about. We had just rowed our way around Taenarum

Point to turn and head north again toward Sparta. Captain Alcimedon routinely kept our distance from the coast to foil raiders, but rounding the tip had brought us in closer. As we rowed past a jutting spur of land, I could see a man lighting a fire on the beach.

The captain joined me on the stern deck soon afterwards. He lifted his head and sniffed. "What's that?"

I gestured to port, where the spur of land was sliding past. "A man was lighting a fire on the beach back there. He must have used some wet wood — it was smoking quite a bit."

He turned to look. A plume of dark smoke was drifting into the sky from the beach in our wake. Concern spread across his face. "You should have told me," he said, frowning. "Come quickly."

He led me into the hold beneath the rear deck. "Grab that and bring it up top," he said, pointing at a wooden box. I struggled up the ladder with the box under my arm as he grabbed a pitcher and followed me up.

The box was filled with arrows, the shaft of each wrapped behind the head with a length of gauzy cloth. He pulled the stopper from the pitcher he had brought up. "Can't dip these in advance," he said. "They dry out." He spread a large cloth on the deck, took an arrow from the box and dipped it, point first, into the pitcher. It came out dripping with a familiar, pine-scented liquid that looked like honey.

"Boiled pine tar, and a few other things," grunted the captain as he laid the first arrow on the cloth. "Dip them like this.

For Zeus's sake don't get any on yourself, or on the deck."

I continued dipping arrows while he stood to watch anxiously over the loose stern rail, taking care not to lean on it. I wondered idly why he didn't fix it. "What is it, Captain?" I asked as he scanned the horizon.

"That smoke," he said. "Another raider trick. A man on the beach sends up dark smoke as we pass to signal a ship hidden just ahead. If I'm right, they'll be just behind that headland," he said, pointing to the promontory to port. "If I'm wrong, no harm done. But I'm mostly right," he added darkly.

A moment later his expression changed. "Rowers, double time," he shouted. "Raiders behind us!" I stood up to look over the railing and saw a ship emerge from cove behind the headland.

"Here," said the captain, pressing a bow into my hand. "I wish we had more bowmen, but we work with what we have." He whistled for the bow lookout, who scrambled across the benches to reach us. "Davos," he said, "you'll present and light. Alexi and I will shoot." Davos, familiar with the task, began dipping more arrows.

The captain and I watched the ship angle closer to us. "Don't fire until I say," he said. The ship was now close enough to see the two men in the bow holding ropes.

"Can you shoot an arrow that far?"

"I think so," I said uncertainly.

"Okay, Alexi. Bows up. Davos, start loading. Me first. Alexi, watch."

Davos took the arrow he had just dipped and notched it onto the captain's bow, carefully holding it in mid-shaft to avoid the pitch. Picking up the ship's fire pot, he pulled off the bronze cover and held the flame under the arrowhead. The tar-soaked cloth caught fire instantly. The captain fired in almost the same instant, but the arrow splashed into the water beside the raider ship.

I realized Davos was beside me with an arrow and held up my bow. He notched it on and lit it. "Shoot!" said the captain. Anxious about missing, I drew too quickly. The arrow fell in the sea ahead of the ship.

"Again," said the captain urgently. "Don't wait to see where it falls. Keep firing." He released another arrow, which fell short of its mark too, as did my next try.

Starting to feel desperate, I thought about hitting seagulls on the wing with rocks, as I'd needed to do sometimes for dinner, back in Troy. This had to be easier — that boat was as big as a thousand seagulls, and it wasn't flying. What direction would I throw a rock to hit a seagull sitting where that ship was? Focusing on that thought as Davos lit my next arrow, I angled the bow into the sky and fired.

A cheer came up from behind me. "Well done, Alexi!" the navigator hissed in my ear. I turned to see two raiders on the centre rowing benches leap up to beat at something on the seat between them. Even so, they'd remembered to ship their oars first to avoid fouling the others.

"Again!" said the captain, as his arrow landed on their

foredeck. I held up my bow to take another and concentrated on where I would throw to hit the foredeck, but overshot and hit the stern deck, almost at the feet of their steersman, who leapt to his feet in alarm. Captain Alcimedon's arrow was in the air almost before mine had landed, and struck the foredeck again. We were getting the rhythm now, and had arrows arcing through the air one after the other. I couldn't see any fire, but some of the arrows must have been landing. Smoke was rising from several places, men dashing around with rags to beat the fires out. Remembering my desperate struggle to do the same thing, back during the Cicone attack, I could almost have felt sorry for them, if they hadn't been trying to rob and murder us.

Despite our arrows, the raider ship had crept up on us, close enough now to see expressions. The men with the ropes in the bow began swinging them. "Grapples," the captain grunted. "Don't let them hit you."

It didn't take long to find out what a grapple was. The men released them simultaneously and they flew through the air at us. The first fell short, but the second whistled past me to land on the deck. It was a heavy bronze triple hook, its tines pointed in three directions. Before Davos could grab it and throw it overboard, the man on the far end had pulled the rope taut, hauling the hook back toward him, searching for something to grab and hold. I leapt out of the way as it rattled past me along the deck, sliding up to catch on the rear rail. The man pulling the rope grinned fiercely and gave it a tug . . . and pulled off the rear railing of our ship. His triumphant expression turned to dismay.

Captain Alcimedon laughed out loud. "I love watching their faces when it does that," he said, as Davos lit another arrow for him. "I keep that rail loose just for that. They can't help wasting their time trying to grapple it. Shoot, shoot!" he urged, as Davos reloaded me. "We're a long way from winning yet. Shoot!"

I paused for a moment. Their fire men were too efficient, putting out arrows before the fire could spread. This close, could I hit somewhere that they couldn't reach? Aha. I tilted the bow downward and shot. The arrow struck the outside of the hull, an arm's length below the rail. The hull would be wetter than the deck, but harder to put out, if it caught.

There was a flicker of flame. Yes! I'd struck the dry hull, just below the deck line. A moment later, the flicker had climbed to their bow railing. The two grappling men, still hauling their grapples out of the water on their long ropes, hadn't noticed. One of the firemen elbowed them out of the way and tried to reach the spreading flame. He couldn't, and leaned over the railing, his back to us as he tried to beat out the flames. At that instant, Captain Alcimedon made a lucky shot and hit him in the back.

He dropped into the sea and was shouldered aside by their keel. His body began to bob along the port side of their ship. The port rowers cursed as their oars struck something, then let rip oaths as they discovered what it was. The port oars fouled as the men dropped them, and the ship slewed to the side and stopped while they struggled to retrieve his body.

"Good idea, Alexi," said the captain. "You've taught me a new trick. Now keep firing. I think they're giving up."

We shot off a few more fire arrows but the raiders were falling back, pausing to retrieve their fallen man. From this distance I couldn't tell if he was dead or not.

"I don't like to do that," said Captain Alcimedon.

Surprised, I glanced at him. "Oh, not for that reason," he said, catching my look. "I'd cheerfully kill every mother's son of them. Keep the seas safer, too. No, I don't like to because if they'd caught us, they wouldn't just sell us as slaves. They'd kill us all, slowly. Or do things that would make us wish we were dead." He mentioned a few details that made the hair all over my body stand up. Surely nobody would do that.

On shore that evening, I helped the captain replace the section of railing. It turned out he had several spares already cut and planed in the hold. "I don't mind saying, Alexi, that I was a bit worried," he said. "I had a few tricks left but they're more as a last resort."

"I guess we were lucky they didn't use their fire arrows on us," I remarked.

"What? Oh, not a chance," the captain replied. "Raiders never use fire arrows. Might damage the cargo." He hammered the new rail section into place onto the short bronze nail stubs sticking up from the railing posts. "There. Looks firm, but it pulls off with a sharp tug. The grapplers always fall for it."

"Why didn't we put up the sail?" I asked.

He shook his head. "That's just what they were hoping," he said. "The wind was onshore today, remember? Putting up the sail, we'd have to go with the wind, which would have meant turning in toward shore. They would have followed us. Close in to shore, we couldn't manoeuvre, and they'd have been on us with grapples and boarders."

We escaped three more raider ships over the next two months, twice through a head start, and a third time with some well-aimed fire arrows that made them drop their chase quickly. By the time we had worked our way up the coast to the Eurotas river mouth, I'd seen more raiders than I wanted to in my lifetime.

"Lacaedemon — what some folks call Sparta — is a long ways inland," Captain Alcemidon explained as his crew offloaded some sheets of tanned leather. "Seagoing ships can't navigate the river, our keels are too low. Talk to the boatman there," he said, gesturing toward a grizzled sailor nearby. "He'll take you up river to Sparta. Fair winds, Alexi."

"Fair winds, Captain."

I came up behind the sailor he'd pointed to, supervising three men loading hides into his boat. "Uh, sir?" I began. "My name's Alexi. Will you —"

"Don't take passengers," he grunted, without turning his head. "Clear off."

Why were ship's captains like this? I stood for a moment,

scrambling for a reply, when he turned toward me. "What did you say your name was?"

"Alexi. Short for Alexias."

He looked at me again, and his weather-beaten face softened. "Alexi. My son's name. Not much to you, is there?" He shrugged. "All right, come on. We'll take you. You'll work your passage, mind."

I scrambled on board and began helping to stow the hides.

"What did you say to him?" one of the other sailors asked me quietly. "He never takes free freight."

On the second evening, as I shared their meal of hard cheese and bread soaked in wine, I ended up sitting on a log next to the captain, who was drinking heavily. Looking for something to say, I asked about his son.

He spat into the fire. "Dead. He's dead now. That war in Troy, it was. Went away to it, but he never came back."

"At least he died fighting," I said, feeling awkward.

"Died fighting?" he grunted. "I'd take a live son over a dead hero. And now I don't even have his body to put to rest. How's he getting to Hades now?" A tear trickled down his cheek, belying his gruff tone.

He sat for a while, brooding. "I hate 'em," he announced suddenly. "Hate 'em all." Trojans, I assumed, but I was wrong.

"Them fancy men in the palace, they took my boy from me. Promised riches, glory, slaves. They made it so he'd be daft not to go. And now my poor boy's dead in some foreign place. I've got no son to pass my life to. And his ma's dead these five years now, too, of heartbreak. And for what?" He glanced upriver in the direction of Sparta. "So those men in their *palace*" — the word was filled with scorn — "can get rich." The other sailors murmured agreement. He took a long drink from a wine skin, put it down and crept off to his bedroll to sleep, leaving me sitting in silence beside the dying fire. I'd always thought that the Greeks had won the war, but the more I saw of the Greek lands, the more I had my doubts.

A few mornings later, the boat pulled up to a river dock at the foot of the hill on which Sparta stood. I helped unload the hides, but rather than wait while the carters bargained, I set off up the road on my own. In contrast to Mycenae, which had sprawled over the hillside like a drunkard across an ox cart, Sparta seemed carefully planned and organized. The city wall was squared off and solid, the mortar between its stones fresh and well maintained. Where Mycenae had seemed gloomy and menacing, Sparta seemed taut and alert. I strode up to the main gates, which were closed, and was about to knock when I spotted the smaller, man-sized door in the wall just to their left. I stepped through.

An efficient-looking guard in armour stood just inside. "State your business," he said crisply.

What had Orestes said? Oh, right. "I bring greetings from Orestes, son of Clytamnestra and nephew of the queen," I said.

The guard looked dubiously at me. "Look," he said. "You seem honest, or too dull-witted to be dishonest, so I'll give you some advice. *Never* mention that you know the queen, okay? Quick way to land your head on a spike. Now, I didn't hear you the first time. You were saying?"

I thought quickly. "Um, thanks. What I said was that I have a message from the nephew of the king of Sparta."

"That's better. I'll send a runner to the palace and see if the king wants you as a guest, or a meal for his dogs."

The message must have been well received, as I was shown up to the palace by an old slave woman. The palace was, as usual, in the centre of town. Every second household seemed to have a woman washing down the door or sweeping the street. There were many young women out, but few men, and most of them were older.

I was shown to a small but comfortable room in the palace, not unlike the one I'd been given at Mycenae. As I sat on the bed, a slave girl of about sixteen came in with a new tunic for me and a basin in which she washed my feet, but looked down and mumbled nervously whenever I asked her about the other slaves. An equally unhelpful old woman brought my dinner on a tray.

Why were they all afraid to talk? When the old woman left with my tray, I stepped out behind her. Surely someone in the serving areas would talk to me. I followed her along the hallway and down some winding stairs, only to encounter a guard at the bottom.

"State your business," he said coldly.

A guard on the slave areas? That was strange. I fumbled for

an answer. "I'm just going for a walk. After dinner, I mean."

"No one enters the slave quarters without the king's permission," said the guard flatly.

"I'm a palace guest," I said. "I didn't know."

"Guests are to remain in their room to await the king's pleasure," said the guard, as if repeating a rule drilled into him.

I began backing up the stairs. "Right," I said. "I'll get back to my room. Wouldn't want the king's pleasure to have to wait."

I retreated to my room, and there I stayed, other than visits to the small garderobe at the end of the hallway, for four days. When the knock came on the fourth evening, I was almost crazy with boredom. At least in the dungeon at Mycenae there had been my fellow prisoners and the occasional rat for company.

I opened the door to a short man with a well-oiled beard and carefully greased hair. "The king desires the presence of the messenger from Mycenae in the royal dining hall," he intoned.

Thanks to Arsinoe, the treacherous old slave woman back in Mycenae, I knew how to fasten a chiton in court fashion. He looked down his nose at me anyway — no small feat for someone barely taller than me — but kept his thoughts to himself. "You may follow me."

I was led to a large hallway and the inevitable set of double doors, which opened to his knock. "A messenger from Orestes, son of the king of Mycenae and nephew of the king of Sparta," he announced self-importantly. I squirmed in discomfort. Somehow, my message of greeting from Orestes had gotten twisted into something grander.

I squared my shoulders and walked into the room.

The room was a dining hall, but to my surprise there was only a single person in it, a round-faced man in a simple yellow chiton sitting at the far end of a long table, evidently meant for a larger crowd. Was he King Menelaus? I couldn't see the queen anywhere. Besides, he didn't seem dressed for it. There were several other stools along the table, one at the extreme far end, and some on either side. Was I supposed to sit down, and if so, where? I felt a sweat start on my forehead as I realized how little I knew about court etiquette.

The man at the table made things easier. "Come in! Come in!" he shouted, gesturing at me with a goblet. "Chrisoman-theus, thank you, you may go." The man who had shown me in bowed deeply and backed out the door.

"Insufferable little man, but he keeps things together for me," the man at the table said to me. "I'm King Menelaus. Have a seat." He gestured to the stool closest to him. "Don't bother sitting down at the far end, I know protocol demands it but it's just awkward."

I came closer and got a better look at him. About fifty, I guessed. With his red nose and broken cheek veins, he looked like a serious drinker. He seemed cheerful, though. Now, how should I address him? "My thanks, Your Highness," I began, settling myself on the stool he'd indicated.

"Stop right there," he interrupted. I froze, half-seated, and he laughed. "No, go on, sit down. I meant skip the whole 'Your Highness' and 'great king' stuff. Not when there's only two of us. 'King Menelaus' or 'Archon' will be fine; I expect that's what you'll be comfortable with. Drink?"

It took me a moment to follow his change of direction. "Uh, yes, your, that is, King Menelaus. I mean, Archon."

He reached over and clapped me on the back. "You're halfway there." He rang a bell and a slave girl came out with a glass of wine. I took a sip and nearly spat it out. It was cold!

The king laughed at my reaction. "Unusual, isn't it? I have ice quarried from a mountain north of Delphi in the winter and stored for the summer in an ice house nearby. We use it to chill wine and fruit. Refreshing, don't you think?"

I took another uncomfortable sip but nodded politely.

"Now," said the king. "What's your message?"

This was going to be awkward. "Orestes, son of Clytamnestra and Agamemnon," I began, "sends his greetings."

The king waited.

"And he, um, would like to invite you to come and visit," I improvised. "Once his kingship is settled," I added. The last thing Orestes needed right now was King Menelaus showing up as a guest before he had retaken the throne.

King Menelaus waited. "And?" he prompted.

"Actually," I swallowed nervously, "that's it."

The king frowned. "That's *it*?"

I nodded.

A change came over his face. His smile melted away, leaving behind a suspicious stare. His cheek twitched, and his head turned slowly until I could see only one eye, staring down his cheek at me. What had I said? I sat, frozen to my seat by his gaze, as the silence stretched.

A noise of crockery came from the room next door. The king's head snapped around, and the suspicious expression vanished. He turned back to me and smiled. "Well, then, if that's the message, let it be so! I've had many a worse one, I can tell you." He rang the bell again. "Let us eat."

A moment later, a door in the side wall opened and a servant girl brought out a platter. She wore a pale blue chiton of some expensive fabric, and her hair was swept up from her neck in an regal hairstyle. She walked oddly, with tiny footsteps.

As she bent to put down the platter she was carrying, I gasped, leaping to my feet. I knew her — it was Helen! I'd seen her a few times back in Troy, where she had been married to Paris, one of King Priam's sons, but even after one glimpse I could never have forgotten her. She had a beauty that Aphrodite herself would have envied. King Menelaus must have brought her home as a slave after Troy fell.

I froze again as I caught King Menelaus's look. At my reaction, he had twisted his head and pinned me once again with that terrifying, one-eyed stare. I sat back down, very slowly. Helen had put the platter down and was hobbling back to the doorway, unaware of the scene behind her.

After what could have been a lifetime, the king blinked and looked around as if puzzled by Helen's disappearance. Eventually he turned back to me. "Know her already, do you?" he asked, his tone casual.

"Know her?" I echoed, stumbling for words. I didn't need the gate guard's warning to know not to admit it. "No, Archon. I was just surprised at such a, well, beautiful slave. Are all your slaves so attractive?"

He laughed again. "If only! No, she's special. Very special." He rang his bell again and she came to the doorway.

"Come out, Helen. Let our guest see you."

Helen hobbled back out, her expression reluctant, and I realized that her ankles were tied together, limiting her to tiny steps.

"Good girl. Turn around. Let our guest see you." Menelaus gestured. "You've got an excellent eye, messenger. She's a beauty, all right. And she's very obedient, as you can see. Does what any man asks."

Helen began to sob. "Menelaus . . . husband . . . please! Why do you keep —"

Menelaus sprang to his feet, knocking over his high-backed chair. "The kuna will not speak!" he roared, pointing at her. "If it wishes to keep a tongue in its mouth it will say nothing!"

He picked up his chair and sat down calmly. "Striking, isn't she? I have to keep her hobbled or she'd bolt." He leaned toward me confidentially. "She did once before. Very awkward. All sorts of trouble to get her back." He sat back. "Would you like her? I'll send her to you after dinner."

I didn't need to understand court etiquette to know that this would be a bad idea. "Thank you, Archon, but I think I'm a little tired. In fact after dinner, I —"

A frown twitched across the king's face. "Don't be silly," he said. "I insist."

The rest of the meal left me sweating, saying as little as possible and choosing my words with care. Eventually, the king stood up.

"Good night, messenger." He gave me a long wink and strode off through a side door without a backward glance, and I found my own way back to my room. Was this what the captain of the *Sappho* had meant about palace intrigue? Life on the streets of Troy had never prepared me for anything like this.

There was a knock at the door. It was her, flanked by two guards. She staggered as they threw her into the room but caught her balance. The reluctance on her face mirrored my own thoughts. All the same, she was Helen, Paris's war bride from Troy, alone in my room, and the most beautiful woman I had ever imagined. Her flawless cheeks and eyes had developed a few creases since I had seen her in Troy, whether from stress or age, but to her face they gave a depth and character that only made her more alluring. Regardless, whatever strange game Menelaus was playing, I had to escape it.

"Look, uh, Hel —" I began but stopped as she interrupted.

"Sit here, master," she said, her tone neutral. She took my arm and guided me to a stool. "Allow me to massage your shoulders, master."

Without waiting for agreement, she came around behind me and began to rub my shoulders. She leaned down toward my ear. "I recognize you," she whispered.

Startled, I turned my head to say something but she shushed me again. "Don't move!" she whispered, bending toward my ear as though applying pressure to my shoulders. "The guards are watching us through the panels. Follow my lead. Don't touch me, whatever you do."

If it had been hard to relax before, it was impossible now. She worked at my shoulders for a moment longer and spoke again, loudly enough to be overheard. "Master, there's a tender spot, here on your neck. Let me blow on it."

She bent down. "It's too hot in here," she whispered in my ear. "You want to take a walk in the garden."

It took me a moment to take her meaning. "Uh, I'm sorry," I said. "It's too hot in here. I need to go outside. Can you take me there?" That wasn't right. She was a slave. "I mean, show me the palace garden, slave," I said, more loudly.

Helen nodded obediently and led me out of the room to a garden outside the palace. The sun had set but the garden was still lit by its fading light. "We can talk safely here, if we're quiet."

"How do you know me?" I asked.

"You look like a healer I once knew. Back in another life." She frowned. "Aristides. Of . . . Heraklion."

She looked at me thoughtfully. "I don't know how his son could be here. He was Trojan." She frowned. "You're not Greek at all, are you? You speak almost with an accent of the eastern islands, but it's not quite right. You're Trojan!"

I felt my eyes widen, but she continued. "Don't worry. I can tell only because of my time in Troy. And I won't let on. Apollo knows, there's no love lost between my husband and me."

"Shouldn't you say 'Aphrodite knows?'" I asked. As the goddess of love, she was the one people used for such comments.

A frown crossed her unbelievably perfect brow, somehow making her, if that were possible, even more attractive. "I won't let *her* name pass my lips," she said bitterly.

I wasn't sure how much time we had. "Helen," I said quickly, "You're right. I'm Trojan. I'm looking for my sister. Taller than me, straight dark hair, grey eyes like mine. Slender. I think she was enslaved the night that Troy fell. Have you seen her?"

Helen's lips pursed in thought. Gods, she was attractive. Trying to talk to her was like trying to talk in the midst of a stampede. No matter how hard I tried to listen, my attention was drawn by the way her lips moved. Her eyes. Her scent. Gods. I forced my attention back to her words.

"I'm quartered with the slaves," she was saying. "There's no one here like that." I felt a sharp pang of disappointment.

"There are a lot of Trojan slave women here, but not her." She looked at me sympathetically. "But there are other citadels. She might be in one of them. If she's still alive."

I felt my face fall.

"If she's pretty, they'll try to keep her alive," Helen said reassuringly. "Besides, it's — stop that," she said suddenly, glancing down.

Startled, I looked down to see my hand almost on her hip. I yanked it back.

She sighed. "It's not your fault. I have that effect on men. I used to like it, when I was younger. But if you give in to it, you'll die."

"Die?"

"My husband, Menelaus. He's crazy with jealousy. Since he brought me back from Troy he's kept me as a slave. That's why the guards watch your chamber. If you'd touched me, they would have told him, and you'd be dead."

I stared at her, trying to think through the fog of attraction assailing my senses. "So, sending you to me tonight," I said slowly. "It was a test?"

Her helpless shrug made me weak in the knees. "No," she replied. "Or yes. I don't know. And I don't know who he's testing, if anyone. All I know is he had one young man run through, two years ago. For holding my hand. He made me watch."

I would have said anything to keep her talking. "Why won't you speak Aphrodite's name?" I asked.

She frowned again, distracting me with the perfect line of her eyebrows.

"... curse *she* put upon me," she was saying. "All for a golden apple that she's surely lost. The worst of it is that even though Paris is dead, I have to love him forever."

I recoiled, and she caught my look. "You'd do the same in my place," she said. "You don't think so, but you would."

She saw my bewildered look. "It was a beauty contest. Hera, Athene and *her*. Zeus wouldn't judge them. Very wise of him. He sent them to Paris, a prince of Troy, and very good looking. But *she* bribed him. She promised him the most beautiful woman on earth. That's me," she added unnecessarily.

"Paris, that utter fool," she said bitterly, "he took her bribe. From that moment on, Troy was doomed. She worked her curse on me, so that the moment I saw Paris, I would fall in love with him. Even though he was a rancid, self-absorbed goatherd with the intelligence of a frog.

"He could have arranged to meet me in private, to sneak into the palace, to leave no trace of where I had gone. Or even to stage my murder. Menelaus would have searched for me and given up. But no, Paris had to come for an official visit with servants, courtiers, gifts, slaves."

Her voice turned wistful. "Gods, the moment I saw him, I was his. I could no more resist him than stop my breath. Even though I could already see just what he was, vain, idiotic and utterly conceited.

"Menelaus, my trusting, foolish husband, left us alone while he went off to negotiate a treaty somewhere. Paris and I, we ran off the next night. He thought it would be a good idea to take most of Menelaus's treasury, so we stole that too, and sailed back to Troy."

She turned to look at me. "So now you know. And I will be

remembered as the most faithless hussy in the history of womankind. Do you want to know the saddest, most tragic part of all?"

I shook my head wordlessly.

"Paris was killed at Troy. But if he could somehow walk into this garden today, I would still abandon everything for him, even if I knew it would start another war more terrible than the first. That is my curse. That is why *her* name will never pass my lips."

She began to sob. Overwhelmed, I brought my arms up around her, stroking her hair as she buried her face in my shoulder.

There was a shout. "Aha! I knew you couldn't be trusted!" We sprang apart to see King Menelaus charging down the path at us, followed by two guards. "And you, messenger. You're after my wife after all!"

"Menelaus, please!" Helen pleaded. "He's just a boy!"

"Your friend Paris was just a boy," Menelaus snapped, pushing her away. "Even locked up with the slaves you find men to beguile. Guards! Take him to the dungeon. We'll hold a public execution in the morning." He looked back at her. "That will teach you to romp in the garden with young men!"

CHAPTER EIGHT

Marked for Execution

THE GUARDS DRAGGED me downstairs and threw me into a dungeon. Their torches gave me a brief glimpse of the filthy cell, its edges sprinkled with mouldering straw, before the heavy door slammed shut.

I lay there most of the night, listening to rustling and squeaking all around me in the blackness. Twice, something scampered over my leg, and once, I leapt up as I felt an experimental nibble at an exposed bit of skin.

I had lain awake like this once before, on the night the Greeks took Troy, as I hid in a filthy culvert under the road. That time, I hadn't known what was coming. This time, there was no doubt. I wasn't sure which was worse.

After drifting in and out of sleep a dozen times, I was awakened by a noise. The dungeon door was pushed open, and two guards came in. They tied a sack over my head and dragged me out. I was led through some corridors and shoved down onto a chair. My hands were whipped around and tied expertly behind me.

"Stay," said one. A door closed behind them.

And then, nothing. This was it. I made quiet apologies to my sister, Melantha, who I would never rescue from slavery. And to Helen, whose situation I had made even worse. And to Lopex, Pharos, Deklah, and all the Greeks who had perished in the shipwreck. Would it be beheading, I wondered, a quick stab with a sword, or would they cut my throat as I'd seen the Greek warriors do? They said that some Greeks killed their victims by pulling them into the air with a rope around their neck. I hoped that wasn't what they did here. It sounded slow.

A door opened. Footsteps walked across a stone floor and stopped nearby. There was the scrape of a chair being pulled up and a moment later, a voice.

"You're the messenger from Mycenae."

There wasn't much to say to that.

"The king wants you executed." A man's voice, not young. "For making eyes at his wife, I presume."

Did the voice sound familiar? Impossible. This was some sort of trick.

Then the voice said something that startled me. "Have you found your sister Melantha yet?"

I twitched. "What?" I said, confused. And then came a sudden rush of recognition as I placed his voice, the last one I would have imagined finding here. "Kassander?"

The bag was tugged off my head. Before me, visible in the light of a torch on the wall, stood a completely bald man with a closely-trimmed beard, wearing a simple white chiton tied at the waist with a blue rope, leaning on a cane. He looked very different from the fellow-slave I'd travelled with nearly two years ago, and I felt a sudden doubt. But then I saw his eyes, and my doubt was gone.

Kassander reached behind me with a knife and cut the hide rope binding me to the chair. I stood up. "There," he said. "Now we're even."

"Kassander!" I exclaimed, giving him a hug. The last time I'd seen him had been on the island of Helios, as he slipped away from the Greeks who were preparing to kill him as a traitor.

He hugged me back awkwardly. "I'm sorry about the hood," he said. "When I heard that someone like you was in the dungeon, I had you brought here. But I didn't want you to know too much until I was sure of you. When you responded to Melantha's name, I knew."

"What would you have done if it hadn't been me?" I asked, curious.

"Sent you back for execution, of course," he replied. "I don't thwart the king unless I have to." He saw my puzzled look. "I'm his advisor."

"But you were on the island of Helios!" I exclaimed. "How did you get away?"

He walked over to the table where a pitcher stood with two rough clay cups. Leaving his cane against the table, he poured some wine into each and handed me one.

"I have my fellow Greeks to thank for that, I suppose," he said. "I knew I'd need a way off the island, so while you and the Greeks were dealing with the cattle, I crept up through the surf and took the ship's skiff from the beach. In the panic to get away the next morning, nobody noticed. Lopex knew, of course."

"Lopex?" I asked, puzzled. "What do you mean?"

"He knew all along who I was. Did you notice how he never gave me tasks that would put me close to the other soldiers? I expect he was counting on you to free me, that night on the island of Helios. Thank you for that, incidentally."

I felt myself floundering. Lopex had known? As if reading my thoughts, Kassander went on. "I saved his life in the war. Lopex isn't one to forget a debt."

"Bu . . . the king's advisor? How did you do that?"

"I filled the bottom of the skiff with drinking water, as much as I dared, and rowed out after you left. A trading ship picked me up and brought me here. King Menelaus needs a cautious, balanced advisor, and I think he understands that, when he's sane. It wasn't hard to talk my way in." He pointed to his bald head. "I keep this shaved so he won't know me from our time at Troy. The cane helps too. Now tell me, Alexi. What happened after you sailed from the island? How did you become a messenger from Mycenae?"

I shuddered, remembering. "We were shipwrecked," I said hesitantly. "A cloud followed us as we left." Had I really seen that giant eye, glaring at us from the cloud? I decided not to mention it. "Thunderbolts from the cloud destroyed the ship, and hunted down the men in the water."

He nodded sombrely. "I'm sorry. They were brave men. Did anyone else survive? How about Lopex?"

I shook my head. "I can't see how. I only got away because Phaith, the shepherd girl on the island, rescued me." I filled him in quickly on all my travels since, searching for my sister.

He put his *kylix* down on the table. "Thank you, Alexi. You may not know it, but in my position, information like this is useful. Now for you. You need to leave, quietly."

"But — won't the king notice? He seemed pretty mad at me."

Kassander shook his head regretfully. "He's not just mad, he's insane. Understanding that makes him easier to control. Today, I'll tell him that the auguries were bad. Tomorrow, I'll say Artemis would be angered if we sullied her feast day. After a few days, he'll forget."

Kassander pulled a ring from his finger and handed it to me. "I suggest heading west to Pylos. From what I've heard, King Nestor brought home nearly a hundred slaves from Troy.

He's wise and trustworthy, and you can be honest with him. This ring will be a good guest-gift, and will prove that you came from here."

"That reminds me," I said. "I think I made things worse for Queen Helen."

He looked at me. This was embarrassing. "She was crying. I . . . put an arm around her. Well, both arms."

Kassander nodded. "I'll sort it out. Menelaus is savage with her. No beatings — he won't risk her looks — but constant humiliation, ever since he brought her back from Troy. I do what I can to make things more comfortable for her. She tells me anything the slaves hear." He paused. "Never trust slaves, Alexi. They'll inform on you if they can. And in particular, don't tell them you were a slave yourself."

"Why not?"

He sighed. "Human nature, Alexi. When I was young, I used to catch crabs with my father. He never covered the bucket, and one day I realized why. As soon as one of them tried to climb up the side, the others pulled it back in.

"Most people like nothing better than to catch someone else climbing out of the muck and pull them back. Don't tell them you were a slave." He thought for a moment. "In fact, don't go by your own name or profession. Pick another."

I thought about it and recalled the name of the priest at Delphi. "Theoclymenos." Then, thinking of what had gotten me out of the dungeon at Mycenae, I added, "seer."

His eyebrows rose, but he nodded. "Not a bad choice. Keep

your predictions vague. If asked, you're from Argos, where you, let me see . . . killed a man who insulted your family honour. It was a fair fight, but you had to flee his family, who would have killed you." He nodded, testing the story for holes. "People will believe that, and nobody will ask questions."

The road to Pylos, Kassander had warned me, would be dangerous. Since returning from Troy, King Menelaus no longer had the men to sweep the roads clear of bandits. "Sparta lost too many men at Troy. The only thing we've got a lot of is slaves," he'd said. "I wish I could spare you an escort, but I can't have a guard around who knows I let you go. No donkey cart either — you'd be seen leaving."

He'd done what he could, providing me a cloak, my travelling pack, which he'd filled with food and water, and my staff. "Oh," he added, holding something out. "There's this too." It was my sister's knife.

"How did you get this?" I asked. "Ury had it!"

Kassander nodded. "I saw Menem and Skaphos bury him in the cess trench just before you sailed. After you left, I dug his body up, hoping he'd still have the knife." He looked apologetic as he saw my gratitude. "I dug it up because I needed it, Alexi. I never imagined I'd see you again. But here you are."

As I walked along the road from Sparta the next morning, the knife was a comforting weight against my hip, tucked into an inside flap of the travelling cloak. Getting out of the citadel unseen had been easy. I'd hidden in the interrogation room until late the next night, when Kassander had led me to the front gate. He had distracted the guard with some sharp questions about the wine on his breath, and I slipped out, taking shelter for the night inside a small shrine to Athene just outside of Sparta.

I felt a lightness return to my footsteps. I had gotten into Mycenae, searched for my sister and escaped again, and done the same in Sparta. Since Melantha hadn't been in either, she had to be in Pylos, from what Orestes had said. I felt sure of it.

The first two days on the road were easy. Travelling past wheat and millet fields, I was able to hitch rides with farmers returning from Sparta, and find a farmhouse to put me up for the night. While the farmers knew all the classic Greek tales I'd learned from my grandmother, the stories of my adventures with Lopex and the crew of the *Pelagios* left them wide-eyed and eager for me to stay longer, even if I didn't sing my stories as the bards did.

On the third day, the road headed into a mountain valley. The land was still green, but most of the farms were abandoned, reminding me of the empty farmhouses on the road to Korinthos. I took to bedding down in them, making a meal of whatever fruit or olives the farmer had been growing, if they were ripe, and breaking into the rations that Kassander had sent with me when they weren't.

On the evening of the fourth night, I headed for a farmhouse as the sun went down. Like most of the others, it was abandoned, and after a meal of half-ripened pears, I went to the farmer's bed in the back room, only to recoil in shock. There was a body in the bed, or rather, a skeleton. The bones hadn't been disturbed, so wild animals hadn't done it. The farmer must have lived alone and had died, peacefully, I hoped, in his bed. I slept on the kitchen floor that night.

On the road the next morning, I found myself wondering why nobody had buried him. Where was his family? My suspicion grew stronger when I found a second skeleton a few days later, lying as if asleep in a chair by the hearth of another farmhouse.

I'd seen no one else on the road for several days, and wasn't sure I was even on the right road anymore, so it was a relief to spot a small village in the distance one evening. A town meant a place to stay for the night, and someone who could tell me if I was still going the right way.

As I neared the town, I could see an old woman, bent over by a heavy load of sticks on her back, on the road a little way ahead. I was about to call out, but stopped as several people stepped out in front of her. I ducked behind a bush to watch. They were children! About ten of them, including a few girls, they all carried spears or clubs. Their hair was matted, their tunics ragged and dirty. None of them looked older than sixteen.

"What's the password, old woman?" said one, a sandy-haired boy who seemed to be the leader.

"Or are you too old to remember it?" said another.

"Probably forgotten where she lives anyway!" jeered a third.

"You young ruffians," she said, starting to walk around them. "Have some respect for your elders." As she passed, their leader grabbed her shoulders and tripped her, knocking her sprawling to the dirt roadway and sending her bundle of sticks tumbling. She struggled back onto her hands and knees, but he came up and kicked her left arm out, knocking her down again.

Two other children leapt to pin her arms down as the sandy-haired boy put a foot on her back and pushed his spear against her neck. She squirmed, grunting something at him. I watched from behind the bush, appalled. Back in Troy, I'd seen the wilder kids — from the wealthy families, mostly — baiting citizens from time to time, but old people were always left alone. Where were the village elders, the men who should be stopping this?

I waited for a moment but nobody came out. The sandy-haired boy changed his stance, putting pressure on the spear point against the old woman's neck.

I felt a chill. Nobody was going to stop this. I picked up a stone, stood up carefully behind the bush, and threw hard, catching the boy behind the ear. He shouted angrily, looking around, but I'd ducked back behind the bush again. My second stone caught him square in the face, but this time I didn't duck quickly enough. There was a shout as someone spotted me. I turned and ran back down the road as the entire pack set off after me.

Two of them, faster than me, were catching up. Angry cries from the boy I'd hit with the rock spurred them on. A spear whistled past and I dodged off the road but tripped over something and went rolling. The children were pounding up behind me, too close to escape. I backed up against a high stone wall, remains of a collapsed house. Snatching up my staff, I lifted it in the two-handed block position that I'd taught myself.

The children stopped, eyeing me warily. The sandy-haired boy panted up a moment later. "What are you waiting for?" he demanded. "Throw!"

After seeing Greek warriors in battle, I could tell that these children were untrained, their spears nothing more than ashwood poles with knives tied to the end. All the same, two spears came whipping through the air, followed by several more. Twisting to avoid them, I managed to dodge or deflect them all with my staff. They crashed one by one into the wall behind me and fell to the ground. If they'd thrown their spears all at once they would have hit me for certain. As it was, they'd just disarmed themselves.

"You're dead, stranger," shouted the ringleader. "The crows will eat your liver tonight."

"Come on, then," I called back, weighting my voice with all the confidence I could dredge up. "You first," I added, facing him, and took a step forward. They fell back, muttering.

Two of the kids at the back shrieked in sudden pain. As the group spun around to see what had happened, I seized the chance to pick up some fist-sized rocks from around the wall and lob them at the group. Under attack from two directions, they ran off, shouting angrily.

Three men came up over the hill in the gathering gloom, carrying bows. "Nephele told us what you did," said one of them, stopping to pick up the arrows that had missed. "Thank you."

They were older men, none of them less than sixty. "Come back with us," the first one added. "We'll get you some dinner and a safe place to sleep. It's not smart to be out in the open come nightfall."

Their house was close by. One of the men called through the door, and there was a pause until it was opened from the inside. As we stepped through, I could see why. Nephele, the old lady I'd helped, was putting back two crossbars behind the door, blocking it shut. Two other older women were preparing a meal at the hearth nearby. A long table, with space for six, had been set with plates and knives, and one of the women dragged over another stool.

"Young man, that was very brave," said Nephele, coming over to give me a hug. "Thank you. They get worse every day. Did they hurt you?"

"No. Thanks."

She shook her head as she saw my eyes drift to a cut on her cheek. "It's nothing. I'm tougher than those young savages realize."

"Who are they?" I asked. "Why don't their families stop them, or the men of the town?"

Nephele glanced at the other two women.

"That's . . . well, that's a hard story," said one, a lady with curly grey hair who was carrying a loaf of bread to the table. She looked hesitantly around the room.

"Go on, tell the boy," said one of the men, peering out through a narrow window. "He deserves to know."

"There was a war," she began, setting out an extra plate at the table. "Twelve, fifteen years ago, I've lost track. Way off to the east. The palace came and persuaded a lot of our young men to go off and fight. They said it wouldn't be long, six months at the outside."

She sighed. "Our Dimitrios, we'd always expected him to follow his father behind the plow. But he went off to the war, along with the other young men of Amphia. We waited. We kept waiting."

She struggled to keep her composure but her face crumbled. "None of them . . . they were so young . . ." She hid her face in her hands.

A second man turned toward me, his face grim. "What Min is trying to say is that none of them came back. Year after year, the palace came through again. At first it was volunteers, but then it changed. If you could fight, they took you. We lost our two sons that way, Phania and I." His face clouded, and he spat. "All thanks to our *King* Menelaus."

The third woman came over from the hearth and put a warning hand on his arm but he shook it off. "Our two boys, dead in foreign lands, denied a proper funeral, thanks to him."

"Don't, dear," said his wife.

"It's true, isn't it?" he said, his voice rising. "Thanks to our great king, we have no one to leave our land to. No one to work it once we die. Our family line will end here."

His wife choked back a sob. The third man shook his head, glancing at me. "Better stop there, Pyrros. We don't know who this is, now, do we?" He turned to me. "No offense, stranger."

Nephele turned from the soup pot on the fire and changed topic smoothly. "It's a shame our Phaidra went off to Mycenae. That's our granddaughter. She'd be just about your age. You seem like a nice boy."

"Oh, Neph," grunted her husband. "Don't embarrass the boy. Phaidra would be too old for him anyway." He looked up at me. "With no marriageable men left here, the young women all went off to the citadel to find husbands. Now all that's left in Amphia is old folk like us and some kids. Most of the kids formed packs, like you saw today."

I didn't understand. "Packs? Why?"

The woman called Phania answered. "It's been some fifteen years since the war started. Fifteen years, stranger. Without their fathers, the children of the village have grown up wild."

"Rejecting their families," her husband interjected. "Little savages."

Phania shook her head sadly. "And with the young men gone, there've been no marriages either. No babies born since then."

When Nephele's husband spoke again, he sounded defeated. "I don't know what it's like elsewhere, but our village has lost a generation. I'm not sure if Lacaedmonia can ever recover."

That night, the men took turns on watch. "They sometimes attack houses at night," said Pyrros, "but don't worry. They have no strategy, and this house is strong. It's not hard to hold them off."

Perhaps the children had been cowed by their defeat, because nothing happened that night. After breakfast the next morning, I was on my way early, my water skins refilled and some new bundles of meat and cheese in my travelling sack.

"This time of day, you'll be fine. They're never up before noon," Phania advised me. "After that, stay alert. The farther you get from the village, the safer you'll be. The right fork in the village square leads to Pylos."

In the early morning, the village had an eerie, watchful feeling to it. Of the dozen houses, at least half were abandoned. The shutters on the others were closed and bolted. Twice I saw people peering out at me as I passed, a woman and an older man. In spite of Phania's assurance that I'd be safe until midday, I looked around regularly as I walked, but saw nothing.

A little before noon, the dusty trail lifted from the plains and climbed into the foothills of a range of low mountains. I had stopped for lunch under an overhanging tree when a rattle of wheels made me leap to my feet. From around the next switchback, a chariot came rattling down the road at high speed, drawn by two sweating horses. I jumped for the edge, nearly tumbling down the embankment, catching a glimpse of two young men, their hair whipping in the wind as the chariot raced by.

I was clambering back up onto the road when I realized the chariot had stopped. One of the riders, a thin-faced, pale young man with a wispy beard, had stepped off the back and was running toward me.

"Are you hurt? I'm so sorry about that! Here, let me help you." He grabbed my shoulder and pulled me up and onto my feet. "This is terrible! It's our fault. Are you sure you're okay? Can I give you anything? Some wine, perhaps?" he asked, brushing some dust and bracken off my travelling cloak.

I shook my head. "No, really. Thanks. I'm fine."

"I'm so glad," he said, relieved. "We were rushing. I'm trying to find my father. The other men came back years ago." He grabbed my shoulder. "Maybe you've heard something. You're coming from where, Sparta? Did you hear anything about the other warriors? At Troy, I mean. My father —" he broke off as the other man put a hand on his shoulder.

"I don't think we want to burden this traveller with our details, do we, Tel? And I'm sure he doesn't want to trouble us with his own." He turned to me. "I'm sorry about that, stranger. We were careless. We're both relieved that you're not injured, and grateful that you're not angry. How is your food supply? On foot, it's a long journey to the next town."

I accepted a dozen boiled eggs with gratitude, and we shared information about the location of water springs in either direction. "Oh," I added. "After this road leaves the mountains, keep your eyes out for a gang of robbers near the town in the plain. I think you'll scare them off with your chariot, but you never know." Adding that they were children would have sounded silly.

It took me another half month of travel before I made it through the mountains and found myself at the gates of the citadel of Pylos. Unlike King Menelaus in Sparta, King Nestor of Pylos gave me an audience with him that same evening, after he had eaten. I was brought to a pleasant, airy room with frescoes of leaping dolphins along one wall, and a scene from the battle between the Olympians and the Titans on a tapestry hanging from another. King Nestor was sitting on a simple wooden chair behind a table at one end of the room, a silent, regal-looking woman who I took to be his wife by his side. He was a tall man, his hair and beard grey, with a large forehead.

"So," he said as I bowed. "You are a traveller through our lands, and you bring greetings from Menelaus in Sparta."

"Yes, Your Majesty." Unsure what to do, I bowed again.

He gestured to a wooden chair at the side of the table. "Please sit."

"I'm sorry, Your Majesty," I said, thinking of something. "May I offer you this as a guest-gift?" I twisted the ring from my finger.

The king took it and examined it politely. "Thank you. A fine guest-gift. Now tell me. How is King Menelaus?" he asked, his tone casual.

I hesitated. "He is . . . well," I said carefully. "As well as can be expected."

King Nestor studied me for some time. "Quite," he said at last. "And Queen Helen? Had you the pleasure of meeting her too?"

I had the feeling that I was being tested. "Yes, Your Majesty," I said.

"And?"

"She is also well." I paused before adding, "King Menelaus is very . . . concerned for her."

"As well he ought," said the king dryly. He sat up abruptly. "It's clear to me that you have seen them both. You may speak freely, messenger. If the leader of a kingdom bordering mine is compromised, then it is in my best interests to know, and his. I have no designs on his land, I assure you. My interest is stability, of which this region has seen too little these past years."

"Your Majesty," I said, "there's something wrong with Menelaus. King Menelaus, I mean. He keeps his wife, Helen, as a slave, and uses her to trap and execute other men."

The king nodded. "I'd heard rumours. You must have some skill, then, young man, to have avoided being entrapped yourself."

I squirmed uncomfortably. Even after being warned, I'd walked right into the trap.

"No matter," said King Nestor, sensing my embarrassment. "Whatever the method, you kept your head. Your information confirms what I've heard. I pity poor Menelaus. He is as much a victim of the war as Helen or poor Troy itself."

"Your Majesty?" I said, surprised.

"Certainly," he nodded. "Menelaus never wanted war. After Queen Helen ran off, he wanted to send envoys to negotiate her return. It was his brother Agamemnon who went to Troy at the head of an army, shouting challenges at the city walls. He knew the king of Troy could never give in without losing face before his people. And so a mighty nation was lost."

He looked across his wine goblet at me. "Please stay as long as you wish, young man. Your information has been helpful."

The next morning, tying off my travel-soiled chiton the way I used to back in Troy, I mussed my hair, rubbed some dirt under my fingernails and wandered into the serving area of the palace. "They sent me down to find a girl," I said to the red-cheeked woman who was running the kitchen. "Her name's Melantha."

I don't know just what she thought I was, slave or servant, but she hardly glanced at me. "They want girls with names now, do they?" she remarked, watching two girls peeling vege-tables. "Did they say what she looks like?"

"Straight dark hair. Grey eyes. Tall and slender." I kept my own face turned so she wouldn't notice how much that sounded like me. Except the height, of course.

"Watch what you're doing," she snapped at one of the girls. "You're losing half the carrot."

She turned back to me. "Nobody like that down here. If

she's pretty, she might be in chambers. Ask the head chamber-maid. No, that way and up the back stairs. Ask for Ariadne." I turned to go but she grabbed my arm. "Mind your manners up there. Call her ma'am or you'll hear from the back of my hand."

I headed up the back stairs, marvelling. Kassander had been right — if you played the part, people didn't even question you.

It took me most of the day to search the places a slave might be stationed: the kitchen, the chambers, the laundry, the garden, and even the stables, although the Greeks never used women there. But nobody had seen anyone who looked like her.

Back in my room, I slumped against the wall, depression overwhelming me. When she hadn't been at Mycenae or Sparta, I'd been sure I'd find my sister here at Pylos. If she wasn't, I had no idea what to do.

CHAPTER NINE

Who Rows to the Fore

MAYBE I'D BEEN FOOLISH, planning to search all of the Greek lands for my sister. But the Furies, whatever they were, had known. Unless I rescued her, the pool of guilt they had uncovered would never be drained.

I left the citadel the next morning and wandered through the streets of Pylos, trying to decide what to do next. Perhaps I should follow my earlier idea and sign on with a trading ship. Maybe my sister had been sold to a rich fisherman in a coastal village. It wasn't likely, but at least I'd be doing something.

The harbour contained some ten or fifteen fishing boats,

some at the docks, others pulled up on the sand. Discouraged, I wandered back into town and sat down beside a fountain in the town square. A couple of sailors, probably crew from one of the fishing boats, came up for a drink of water.

"Going to top the stores?" one was saying. "Even he'd have to notice if they were half empty."

"You'd think so, wouldn't you?" said the other sailor, bending to drink from the fountain. "But he didn't know enough to check before we pulled from Ithaca!" They both laughed.

Ithaca. Now why did that sound familiar? I couldn't place it, but these sailors, with their talk of topping up stores, couldn't be off a fishing boat. They were from a long-distance ship, and one that sounded like it was leaving soon. I got up to follow them.

They headed to the harbour and north along the beach to a cove where a ship bobbed at anchor. At their whistle, the watchman came out in a ship's dinghy.

I caught up as the two sailors seated themselves on the bench across from him. "Excuse me," I said politely. "Who is the master of that ship?"

The watchman didn't look up. "Who's asking?"

I suppressed my annoyance. "I am Theoclymenos of Argos," I said firmly, using the name that I'd picked with Kassander. "Messenger to the court of King Nestor of Pylos, and his personal guest in the palace."

The watchman's eye took in the finely-woven chiton I had been given at the citadel. "He's not here," he said sulkily.

"Do you know when he'll be back?" I asked, keeping my voice calm.

"Sorry, mate," he replied, his voice suddenly smug. "He didn't say. Could be months." He winked at the two sailors sitting across from him and pushed the dinghy away from the beach with an oar.

"Thank you for your help," I called. "When I dine with King Nestor tonight, I'll tell him just how helpful you've been." I turned away.

"Wait a bit," he called back, suddenly anxious. "Dining with King Nestor?"

I stopped.

"Just having a bit of fun, that's all," he said. "No need to go off like that."

I turned slowly. "Well?"

The dinghy's bow nudged back into the sand. "He's gone to Sparta. Not sure when he'll be back. Next few days, I think."

"Thank you," I said coldly. "When your master returns, send a runner to the palace to tell me."

Not that there was any chance of him doing it. I kept an eye on both the harbour and the cove for the next few days but saw only the fishing boats, returning with the day's catch each afternoon.

A few days later, I was walking down the road that led north to the cove, when a mud-spattered chariot clattered past me. I stepped aside as it passed but it pulled up just ahead of me. A skinny young man hopped off and ran back.

"You!" he exclaimed. "So you made it!"

It took me a moment to place him. It was the young man who had run me off the road on the way to Pylos.

"My name is Telemachus," he went on. "Everyone calls me Tel. Where are you headed? Can we give you a lift? The chariot's meant for two but I'm sure we can squeeze you on."

The second man on the chariot joined us after tying up the horses. "Pysis," the skinny young man said to him, "do you remember? This is the traveller we ran off the road! On the way to Sparta, remember? His name is —" he broke off, realizing we hadn't exchanged names, and turned back to me. "What's your name, stranger? You never told me."

His companion held up his hand. "Tel, remember what we talked about? Don't ask. If someone wants you to know his name, he'll tell you." He looked at me. "Sorry about that, stranger. Tel here grew up without a father. There's no faulting his courage, but he hasn't yet learned how men speak to one another." He punched Telemachus's arm fondly.

Telemachus, who I now realized was a few years older than me, rubbed his arm, embarrassed. "Sorry," he said. "My mother says to guard my tongue or nobody will respect me. You were right about those robbers, you know. Our chariot scared them off. They were kids! Do you need anything? At least let us give you a lift." He paused, apparently for breath.

"Thanks," I said. "My name is —" I hesitated for a second, trying to remember the name I'd chosen — "Theoclymenos, of Argos. Call me Theo."

The charioteer dropped us both at the cove where the ship lay. "Goodbye, Telemachus," said the charioteer, giving him a hug. "I hope you find him. I need to get back. My own father will be waiting to hear from me. Goodbye, Theoclymenos." He climbed back aboard the chariot and rode back toward town.

As Tel whistled to the ship, it came together for me. "You're the master of this ship, aren't you?" I asked.

"That's me," he answered. "I was looking for my father. Were you in the war? You must have heard of him. His name is Odysseus. His men call him Lopex."

I staggered. My old master! I'd known him as Lopex for so long that I'd almost forgotten his real name. Odysseus, the man who had torn me from Troy, enslaving me and forcing me to be part of his terrible adventures. Thanks to him, I'd been only a scream away from death a dozen times. The last time I'd seen him, we were both struggling to survive the wreck of our ship and escape the lightning bolts that were hunting us down in the water. But only I had been rescued.

I lifted my head to see Telemachus peering anxiously at me.

"Are you okay?" he asked. "You look terrible!" His eyes widened slowly. "You know something, don't you? About my father? Please, if you know, tell me!"

I struggled to get my thoughts in order. There was no way I could tell him. That would connect me to Troy and slavery. Who knew what other warriors had returned from Troy, having seen a short, grey-eyed boy among the slaves?

"I'm sorry," I said. "I've heard of Odysseus, of course. Who hasn't? One of the heroes of the Greek —" I caught myself just in time — "the Trojan War."

Telemachus was still looking at me. "What happened? You looked like you'd seen the Furies themselves."

I stiffened again. If only he knew. "Oh, that," I said, struggling to think of an answer. "I was just surprised that you were his son."

He looked at his feet. "I'm not much compared to him, am I?"

"That's not what I meant," I began.

"It's okay," he went on. "They say he made people respect him. I wish I knew how to do that."

"Well," I said, "thank you for the lift. I hope you find your father."

"Where are you headed?" he asked. "Would you like to come back with us to Ithaca?"

That was where I'd heard of Ithaca. Lopex's home island. "Gods, no," I said quickly. "Sorry. I meant to say my path takes me elsewhere."

He nodded. "You'll be welcome if you ever visit." He turned and stepped into the waiting dinghy.

"Here you go, sir," the watchman was saying, patting the rowing bench.

"What?" asked Telemachus.

"It's good luck, sir, for the master of the ship to row himself out on the return trip. Surprised you haven't heard."

I looked at the watchman, but his face was carefully blank. I was about to turn and walk back to the citadel, but stopped. Instead of facing backwards, as rowers did to put their backs into the task, Telemachus was facing forward on the rowing bench, pushing the oars away from him to row while facing forward. I'd seen my old master order his men to do something similar in an emergency, but it looked silly here.

"That's a much better way, sir," said the watchman, winking at the sailors watching from the ship's bow rail. "Rowing to the fore like that. I can't think why we don't all do it that way."

Something rolled over in the depths of my memory. *The one who rows to the fore.* Crazy Cassie had said that. *He will find her.* I watched Telemachus row awkwardly out to his ship, wondering. Even as the first half of her prediction came true before me, I felt as if something was pinning my mind, preventing me from believing her.

But Orestes had said it too, and Orestes, I could believe.

"Telemachus!" I called, waving to him. "I've changed my mind. I'd like to come with you."

Telemachus was the captain, but the sailors, a collection of wiry old men and a few young toughs back from the war, paid him no attention, laughing behind his back and ignoring him to his face. As far as I could see, it was only with the navigator's help that he was able to keep the ship on course at all. But as long as we didn't have any emergencies there were enough experienced seamen in the crew to trim the sail and keep the ship running.

The trip to Ithaca was to take about five days. Telemachus had nobody standing watch, something that left me nervous after my experience on the *Arethusa*, so I volunteered. For the first four days, the only ships we saw were one- and two-man fishing boats.

On the fifth afternoon, I was on watch in the bow when Tel came up and leaned on the rail beside me. "I'll be so glad to see Ithaca again," he said. "I think we should be there to-night. At least, the navigator says so. But I don't know what I'm going to tell my mother," he added. "She would never have let me go. So I went without telling her. I was so sure I could find some news of my father. But now, coming back with no news . . ." He trailed off, peering across the sea as if hoping to spot his father's ship.

I changed the topic, not wanting to think about the last time I'd seen his father. "So what's Ithaca like?"

"Oh, it's a beautiful island," he said. "It's the furthest west of the chain. My father built his palace up high so my mother could always see the sun set over the sea. But these last few years, she's been pretty busy with all the house guests."

"House guests?"

He nodded. "They started coming about five years ago. At first they'd come for a few days or a month and be on their way. But now they come, and they stay." He shrugged. "My mother is a big believer in the whole hospitality duty. *Xenios* and all that. But the truth is —" he lowered his voice to a whisper — "I think she's afraid of what they'd do if she told them to leave. She doesn't even dare to refuse them wine, so they're drunk most of the time."

"Who are they?" I asked.

"Noblemen's sons, mainly. A few princes. A couple of kings that have been deposed, I think while they were away at the war. A few of them are just ruffians. They've come from all over. One's all the way from Attica."

"What are they doing there?"

He looked uncomfortable. "Drinking, mainly. Plus a lot of gambling. Eating too. And pestering the house maids. They make a horrible mess. To tell you the truth, from the way they look at her, I think a lot of them would love to marry my mother, if she stopped waiting for my father." He brightened. "But they're awfully good to me. When I told them I was taking a ship to find news of my father, they gave me lots of advice. Antinous must have told me five times to avoid the Petrikata Strait. He said the Asteris Strait was safer."

That sounded strange. "Why?"

Tel frowned. "You know, I don't think he said. But it's sure longer." He borrowed the navigator's map and unrolled it across the bow rail, showing three long islands running roughly north-south. He pointed to the leftmost. "You see here? This is Ithaca. My father's palace is in the bay on the northernmost point. The big island in the middle is Same. On the right, this is Doulichion."

He lowered his voice. "Don't tell the sailors, but I don't know much about sailing. Me, I would have come north up the Petrikata Channel. Here, between Same and Ithaca. But coming up the Asteris Strait, we're hidden from Ithaca until we're almost there. And we have to cross more open sea too."

That got me thinking. "What would happen if you didn't come back? If this ship was wrecked, for instance?"

Tel glanced around, alarmed. "Don't say that! These sailors are as flighty as pigeons." He thought about it. "Having me there has helped my mother. If I didn't come back she'd be heartbroken. Probably she'd just give up, marry one of the house guests."

He turned to me, his eyes widening as something occurred to him. "You don't think that's what they're doing, do you, Theo? Waiting for my mother to marry one of them?"

I took a deep breath. Had he spent his whole life with his head in a bucket? "Tel, that's exactly what they're doing. Whoever marries your mother becomes king of Ithaca, doesn't he? But what's worse, you've just said that if you never came back, your mother would remarry."

"I guess so," he said hesitantly, "but —"

"Where are we now?" I interrupted.

"Part way up the Asteris Strait, if I'm reading this right." He bent over the sheepskin. "See, that's Same over there." He pointed to a coastline sliding past us to the left.

I wanted to shake him. "Tel," I said firmly, "listen to me. Those men are not your friends. I think they told you to come home this way so they could kill you."

He went pale. "Kill me? I know they can be pretty rude, but —"

"Sail ahead!" the navigator called.

Sure enough, there was a sail ahead of us, too far to make out details yet, but growing larger. After a few moments I could see it was heading straight for us.

The navigator came over. "Sir," he said to Telemachus. "I don't like the look of that ship."

Telemachus peered at it. "Why not?"

"Well, sir, honest ships normally leave a wide berth around one another, so that nobody gets mistaken for raiders. This ship, though, she's bearing straight down on us, and she's under sail and oars both. That's a raider tactic."

Telemachus looked worried. "What should we do?"

"We can't fight them. We should turn the ship around now and outrun them under sail."

"Don't," I said urgently. "That's exactly what they want."

The navigator glanced at me. "And what would you know about it?" He turned back to Telemachus. "We don't have time to argue. Turn the ship and get the sail up."

I took Telemachus by the arm and pointed. "Look at them, Tel. See how narrow that ship is? It's built for speed, and they're already under sail and rowing hard. If they're raiders, they won't even carry water, to keep their weight down. To outrun them, we'd have to mount the mast, raise the sail and turn the ship around. We wouldn't be even half done before they were on us with grapples."

Telemachus looked even more anxious. "So . . . what, then? Should we give up, Theo?"

It took me a moment to remember the name I'd taken.

"Gods, no!" I answered. "Definitely not. What weapons do we have on board? Spears, arrows, shields?"

Telemachus thought. "I saw a few spears in the hold. No bows or arrows."

"Too bad. We could have tried fire arrows, if we had some pitch," I said, thinking of Captain Alcimedon's tactics against the raiders. The Cicones had used the same tactic against us after we'd left Troy.

"Pitch?" Telemachus broke in on my thoughts. "The sailors re-caulked the ship's seams in Pylos. The spare pitch went into the hold."

That was something. I glanced at the other ship. It was still far away, but the sail was already growing against the horizon. "Here's what we have to do. We need them to believe that we think they're friendly so we can get as close as possible."

"Oh, really? How?" asked the navigator, folding his arms across his chest. "Stand in the bow and wave?"

"That's a great idea," I said quickly. "Thanks for offering. When they get closer, wave. Shout. Think of something. We're going to continue on the same course, straight at them."

"But that's a warship! They'll rip through us like a burial shroud!"

"Straight at them," I repeated. "Tel, I want you to prepare the rowers. I'll be on the stern deck. Tell the port side rowers to be prepared to lift their oars straight up in an instant. If I gesture like *this*" — I held my left arm straight out and bent it straight up at the elbow — "the rowers are to lift their oars out *on that side of the ship* as fast as possible. If I do *this*" — I put my right arm up and windmilled it backwards — "reverse direction and row backwards."

"Backwards?" the navigator and Telemachus said at once.

I nodded. "Just as you did in the dinghy, Tel, but facing the other way. Then meet me on the stern deck. Meanwhile, I'll be checking out that pitch. Tel, do we have any goatskins?"

Telemachus nodded. "Sure, in that box." He pointed. "But are you sure? We don't have any arrows —"

I cut him off. "If this works we won't need them." I glanced up at the other ship, which had already cut the distance between us in half. "But we have to be quick."

Collecting three goat skin sacks, I filled them with sticky pitch from the clay jugs in the hold, and stuffed a rag into the drain hole of each, before taking up position on the stern deck.

Tel was walking down the rowing benches, explaining what I wanted, but the rowers looked skeptical, rolling their eyes or just ignoring him.

This wasn't going to work. If the rowers didn't all respond when I gestured, the plan would fail. Once again, my thoughts turned to Lopex. Odysseus, I reminded myself. Bringing his men around after throwing the dead bodies overboard, or in Hades, or after battling the Cicones. Once again, the thought inspired me. I leapt up onto the stern rail.

"Men of the *Neaera*!" I shouted, drawing myself up. "If you want to live, listen to me!"

I had their full attention now, if I could just keep from

falling into the sea. They watched in surprise as I balanced on the stern railing.

"A raider ship is bearing down on us at high speed," I said loudly. "They have the wind of us and we have no time to evade them. We can escape, but only if you do what I say. *Exactly* what I say," I repeated, borrowing Lopex's words from the island of Helios.

"Telemachus has told you what we need from you. But if any man here is afraid, show it now by resting on your oar." Lopex's words had been made for this. Nobody would dare object now.

"The man who is an instant slow to respond will doom his shipmates," I finished. "*Can you do it?*"

Standing on the stern rail had helped. Only someone very sure of their message would risk drowning to deliver it. Convinced, the sailors roared back their agreement.

I leapt down as Telemachus came over to join me. "Here," I said, thrusting the three goat skins into his hands. "Loosen the seams on the bags and tie these ropes around them. Light the rags from the stern fire pot the moment we start to turn."

The other ship was closing, and despite his doubts, the navigator was doing his best, waving and calling to them as if they were old friends. I could see the men on the bow deck of the approaching ship now, holding grappling ropes in their hands as they watched the gap between the ships close. From their puzzled expressions, they wondering why we weren't putting up our sail and running as they'd expected, and why we didn't seem worried that we were about to be rammed.

This was going to be very close. If I got the timing wrong, or if the raiders reacted too fast, they would hit us, and the navigator was right about one thing: at that speed, their ship would slice us in half.

Now. I turned and put my right arm out, windmilling backwards. The starboard rowers followed my gesture and began rowing backwards where they sat. With their oars churning backwards, the *Neaera* turned to starboard instantly, exposing our port flank to the oncoming raiders. Caught off guard, they began their own turn to port to stay on target, but at their high speed, and turning only with their steering oar, they were too slow.

Now. "Starboard rowers!" I shouted. "Standard row!" I worked my right arm the other way and our turn straightened back out again. Our quick turns to starboard and port had shifted us a bare ship's-width to the right, taking us out of the direct path of the oncoming raiders. We were going to slide past them, barely. Taken by surprise, the raiders weren't reacting fast enough.

Now. As we drew abreast of their ship, I put out my left arm and gave the signal for the port side rowers to pull in their oars. There was a cracking and snapping from the raider's ship as the *Neaera* ploughed over their outstretched oars. Expecting to ram us, their rowing master had been caught off guard. A few of their oars were pulled in, some cracked, but most snapped upward as their blades were forced beneath our keel. Shouting, the rowers on the other ship were thrust into the air on their oars or knocked into one another as their oars leapt violently from their grips. The two men in the bow, holding grapples, were knocked from their feet as the ships rubbed against one another.

Now. I signalled Tel to start throwing. He had lit the rags on cue, but hadn't figured out the purpose of the attached ropes. He heaved the first goat skin over the rail like a sack of potatoes. It fell well short of the other ship and dropped into the sea. Abandoning my rowing signals, I ran over and grabbed the second skin, whirled it around on the rope a couple of times and let it fly across to the other ship. It landed on a rowing bench amidships. With its loosened seams, it popped open on impact, spattering the benches and rowers around it with sticky pitch.

No time to watch. I reached for the third bag, but as I picked it up I could see that the second hadn't caught — the rag had blown out as I spun it. One more chance. I snatched up the last bag and ran to the rail. The other ship was almost past us, its stern across from ours, close enough to jump onto. Picking up the final bag, I tilted it until the entire rag had caught and flames were licking at the goatskin bag. I spun it on its rope and heaved it across the gap. It smashed on the stern deck and burst, spilling pitch across the deck and the steersman.

I held my breath. There was a sudden soft whoomf and a flame appeared on the stern deck, spreading quickly in all directions. Running like water, it climbed up the steersman's leg and across his torso where the pitch had stuck. He screamed, letting go of his oar to leap into the water. The shouts from the other ship redoubled as the men scrambled to deal with the spreading fire. Now behind us, the ship slewed to a halt as the rowers leapt from their seats to escape the flames.

I turned back to our rowers, who had almost stopped rowing as they watched. I put my arms out and gestured. "Both sides! Standard row, double time!" I shouted. The port rowers scrambled to extend their oars again, and our ship began to pick up speed. When the rowing was well sequenced, I put down my arms to look back.

Well behind us now, the other ship had lost all headway. Smoke from the fire was sending grey clouds into the sky as the raiders rushed to fill buckets of seawater to put out the flames. A number of oarsmen had jumped overboard to put out their burning clothes.

Tel joined me at the stern rail, and we watched the raiders struggle to put out the fires and retrieve their crew members. "Pysis keeps telling me I don't know how men speak to one another," he said quietly. "If that's how you do it, no wonder I haven't been getting respect."

I shrugged awkwardly. "The rowers could see how urgent it was," I began, but at that moment the navigator joined us at the rail.

"Are you setting to sea again soon?" he breathed, his voice alight with awe. "Because if there's any chance of seeing that again, I'm sailing with you."

CHAPTER TEN

Arrow through the Axes

WRAPPED IN A BEGGAR'S ragged travelling cloak, the stranger leaned against the wall of the hut, asleep. I couldn't make out his age. He was hunched over like an old man, his face hidden by the shadow of a heavy hood, but something about him suggested a hidden strength, a wooden arrow with a bronze core.

Four of us were sitting around a small fireplace in a hut up in the hills of Ithaca. The *Neaera* had arrived at the harbour on Ithaca earlier that afternoon, but instead of going to the palace, Tel had taken me here. "If you're right about our house guests," he'd said as we followed the winding path into the hills, "I think I should talk to our stockman before going up to the palace. He's been with us since before I was born. He'll know what's going on."

The stockman turned out to be a bear of a man with a curly brown beard and a red face. When he saw Tel at the door, he'd swept him into a powerful hug. "Your mother, she's been crying her eyes out since you left, young man." He held him at arm's length for a moment. "But by the gods, it's good to see you." He waved us to the two empty seats around the fireplace. "Have you been to see your mother yet?"

Telemachus looked down. "Well, no. Not just yet. What's been happening, Eumaeus? I mean, since I went away? Have they —"

"You mean, have those dogs forced your mother to marry?" The stockman's voice flickered with anger.

"Well, yes."

"How can you ask? Of course not. But it gets harder every day for her to refuse. Especially," he added, looking directly at Tel, "when her son isn't around to support her."

Tel looked embarrassed. "I was really hoping I could find my father. Or at least news of him. Did you know we were attacked by raiders? Don't tell my mother. I'd better get up there now." He turned to me. "Theo," he said, "let's get going. I'll bring you up to the palace."

The stranger uncurled himself and sat up. "Young Telemachus," he said. "Stay." So he hadn't been asleep. "There is something you must know. It is for your ears alone." His voice was deep and gravelly, but something about it was familiar.

Tel, sitting on the opposite side of the fire from me, glanced over uncertainly at Eumaeus, who shrugged. "Theo," Tel said, turning to me, "do you mind going on without me? Wait, you don't know where it is. Eumaeus, would you mind . . ."

The stockman nodded. "I'll take him up, and tell your mother you're on your way too. It's cruel to leave her worrying."

Tel nodded awkwardly.

"And you, stranger," the stockman added, turning to the hooded man. "Don't be filling this boy's head with a lot of muck. There's been plenty of men have come round claiming news of his father, and Queen Penelope has given them her ear, every one. Don't you be another, d'you hear?"

The stranger nodded slowly. "You have my word, Eumaeus, that I will speak only the truth."

The stockman looked at him for a moment. "I believe you will at that, stranger," he said, and beckoned to me. "This way."

"Palace is what they calls it, around here," Eumaeus remarked as we followed the winding path up the hillside. "But that's just their way. The folks on Ithaca, most of them has never seen a proper palace. This is more what you'd call a great house. My master Odysseus, he built it himself, did you know?"

I said something polite.

"Well, not himself, of course, that'd be silly. But he did all the design, and he measured and made sure it was all done right. He'd have done over the world for that wife of his, Penelope." The shepherd shook his head. "He'd never of put up with this nonsense. He'd clear these men out before you could slap, he would."

Suddenly it was before us in the gathering darkness, a beautiful spreading building of wood and stone, facing west toward the sunset. A cluster of ornate tents stood on the grassy areas to either side. The stockman glanced at me apologetically. "If it's all right with you, I likes to go in the back way. Don't attract so much attention, you see."

He took me around to a small door at the rear. As he led me through a storeroom, I could hear raised voices, and then a loud crash and a burst of laughter. We passed through another storeroom and were suddenly in a brightly lit *megaron*, although smaller and much less opulent than the grand hall at Mycenae.

The room was crowded with men. Some were only a few years older than me, but most were old enough to be fathers themselves. They were clustered at the far end of the room, eating dinner on stools at one of fifteen or twenty small tables. Above us, a railed balcony ran around the top of the room, doors to what would be the women's rooms on the second floor opening from it, and a stairway in a corner. Shields and spears decorated the main floor walls.

Something sailed through the air, shedding its contents as it flew, and shattered against the wall above a large stone fireplace. "Eurymachus," someone shouted, "if that's your best, cut off your hands and spare us!" There was another burst of drunken laughter.

The suitors were throwing earthenware plates laden with

food at the fireplace, spinning them like discuses. I couldn't tell what the goal of the game was, and I was pretty sure they couldn't have told me either. The whole room showed signs of hard use, with smoke damage against the walls from dozens of fires, broken tables and stools, pieces of smashed crockery and scraps of food littering the floor.

Beside me, the stockman shook his head sadly. "Like this every night, it is. No notion of the respect they owes the land or its lady. I'm just sorry this is how a proud house greets you. That reminds me, I've a message to deliver. Sit yourself down. The maids will feed you, we can still do that properly."

I righted a stool and sat down in a darkened corner to watch. It was as bad as I'd heard. Drunken and brawling, they were behaving exactly like the barbarians I'd once thought all Greeks were.

I hadn't been sitting long when two of the suitors, better dressed and groomed than most of the others, peeled them-selves away and sat down nearby. I shrank farther back into the shaded corner to listen.

"Antin," one of them said, "I've just gotten word from my spy in the harbour. That young pup's ship has just put in."

The second man leapt up. "Telemachus? Are you sure?"

The first man nodded. "How could the young fool have evaded them? We told him to come back up Asteris Strait. Did he not listen?"

The second man, Antin, sat down slowly. "That hardly matters now. We need a new plan. Every one of us paid those raiders, so each man here is in it. They'll have to follow our lead now."

"But what can we *do*?" said the first man anxiously. "I have to tell you, Antin, I'm worried. It's not like doing it at sea. If we do it here, she'll know it was on purpose."

Antin's oily smile was like a dungeon door opening. "Haven't you seen the cliffs south of here? There are other deaths than at the hands of sea raiders. When the little fool comes back, we'll arrange an accident. She'll collapse like wet cake when she sees his body, I assure you."

"And what about *him*, Antin? What if *he* comes home?"

Antin shook his head slowly. "Amph, Amph. Surely you don't think Odysseus is going to show up now, after so long? I only wish he would. We've been saying he's dead for years. If he shows up, we could prove it."

The man he'd called Amph looked perplexed. "Prove it?"

Antin smiled again. "There are over a hundred of us. Cut off his head and show it to her. She'd have to believe us then, wouldn't she?"

Amph nodded, impressed. "Now that, I like. She'd cry, but she knows a palace needs a master. We've proven that to her, haven't we?" They both laughed hard, slapping one another's backs before getting up to rejoin the other suitors at their game.

The next morning I was sitting on a stool at one end of the room, eating a breakfast of grapes and cheese that the serving girls had brought in, when the big double doors swung open. Telemachus walked in, followed by the hunched beggar I'd seen in the stockman's hut, leaning on his staff. Something like anger flickered in his eyes as he looked around.

The men in the room stared, astonished, but Antin rushed over immediately. "Telemachus, dear boy!" he exclaimed, clasping his hands. "How wonderful to see you back safely! I must tell you, a few here doubted the wisdom of your task, but I had no concerns. How did your little errand go? Did you hear any news of your dear father?"

"My thanks for your greeting, Antinous," he said flatly. "No, I found no news of my father in Pylos."

Antin's attention was caught by the stranger. "And who is this?" he asked. "Surely you're not bringing a beggar into the house? Get out, you." He reached for the beggar's shoulder.

"Stop, Antinous," said Tel. "He is my guest." He turned to the beggar. "Stranger, make yourself at home. I have to go and greet my mother." I looked up, surprised. Tel's voice had a new ring to it, a confidence I hadn't heard before.

The beggar looked down and his eyes softened. A ragged old hound had limped in behind them and was sniffing his foot. He knelt down to pat the dog's head.

"This should be good," I heard someone say. "That old cur mauls anyone who touches it."

But the dog thumped its tail slowly against the door frame as the beggar fondled its ears. Around me, the suitors looked on in surprise. The dog licked the beggar's hand tenderly and its tail thumped again, more slowly. It slumped to the floor, coming to rest on its side. Its eyes were still open, and it didn't move again.

"It's dead," someone said, shocked.

"It was waiting for something," said someone else, in a quiet voice that carried through the room. "Before it could die."

The room was silent.

"What is this foolishness?" Antin demanded, his voice crackling through the room. "Phemios!" he shouted. "Give us a song! Where is that simpering weakling?"

There was a commotion from the corner as a spindly, ragged-looking minstrel was dragged out from where he'd been curled up. His voice wavered nervously as he began a song of Achilles, hero of the war, and his fingers missed their chords.

"Gentle Phemios!" It was a woman's voice, coming from the balcony above us. I looked up to see an attractive, graceful woman in an ornate robe and carefully styled hair. That had to be Telemachus's mother, the woman the stockman had called Penelope.

"Please ignore them," she said, descending the staircase. "Your sweet voice would not shame Apollo himself. I beg you, sing something to lighten my mood." Phemios smiled at her gratefully and started over. She was right. His voice was beautiful.

Meanwhile, one of the serving maids had brought a plate of beef strips to the beggar, who had taken a seat by the fire.

She slammed the plate down on the table and turned to leave, but the beggar caught her arm. Her eyes widened as he spoke to her and she backed into a table, sending plates crashing to the floor.

"What did you do to her, old fool?" someone shouted.

"Maybe his smell scared her off!" came another voice, to general laughter.

Finally, Telemachus, who had been standing on the stairs with his mother, spoke up. "That is *enough!*" he said. "For years you have abused this house's hospitality, while I could do nothing. But from this moment on, things are different. This honourable stranger will eat with me off our finest plates. I only wish I could horsewhip you all into the street as you deserve, but in this, my father's house, you will at least be civil to my *invited* guests."

An amazed silence fell, only to be broken after a few moments by a loud, ragged voice. One of the suitors, a rounded man with a red face, had lurched to his feet. Although it was only mid-morning, he was swaying drunkenly.

"Good idea," he slurred. "Gold plates for the hobo. And while you're at it, why don't you give him a shot at your mother too? I mean, fair's fair."

Somebody tried to hush him, but he went on. "Wait, I know. He needs a gift for her!" He looked around and spied a cooked calf's hoof on a platter from the previous night. "Stranger, catch!" He lobbed the hoof at the beggar. It thumped against a wall near him. Losing his balance, the man collapsed back onto his stool.

Shaking off his mother's warning hand, Telemachus leapt down the stairs and ran across the room, grabbing the drunken man by his hair and tilting his head back to place a sharp-looking knife at his throat.

"Didn't you hear me, Ctesippus?" he said loudly. "I told you I expected respect for my guest. But you're a foolish drunkard, so maybe you missed it." He lifted the knife and looked around the room. "Do you hear me? The next man who insults my guest, or speaks coarsely about my mother, will face me in combat. I am ready to die, if the gods wish it. Are you?"

I stared at him. This wasn't the Telemachus I'd met back on the road to Sparta. This was a man, alight with an angry confidence. Somehow, he seemed to have grown up overnight.

The suitors could feel it too. As they finished their breakfast in awkward silence, I slipped away to search the palace for my sister. There were about fifty servants and slaves there, either in the palace or smaller outbuildings, but none of them had come from Troy. Mindful of Kassander's warning, I was careful not to admit that I had once been a slave too. Dejected, I returned to the *megaron* late in the afternoon.

That evening, the suitors, waiting for dinner, were standing in a circle, shouting excitedly as they wagered on three fighting roosters. I had seated myself in a quiet corner far from them, when Telemachus's mother Penelope came up and sat near the beggar, who was perched on a stool near the fire, his ragged cloak wrapped around him. He stood up as she approached, but she waved him back down.

"Stranger," she said politely, "you intrigue me. May I sit with you?"

"It would give me pleasure, my lady," he said. His gravelly voice bore the cracks of age, but for the second time, I had to wonder why his voice sounded familiar.

She took a seat on the stool beside him and they both sat, staring into the flames. "I have trouble seeing you as a beggar, stranger," she said quietly. "You hardly seem the type."

"Who among us is what he seems, my lady?" he replied softly, not turning his head.

She sat stiffly for a little while. "My son tells me you're an intelligent man, once the lord of a great manor, who has fallen on hard times."

"That much is the case, my lady," he murmured.

"As such, your insight would be —" she hesitated "— timely. May I ask your advice?"

At his assent, she went on. "My husband Odysseus, who men called Lopex, left me for the Trojan War many years ago. Being a practical man, he said that if he had not come back by the time our son grew up, I should remarry."

"Remarry?" the stranger said softly. "Abandon your marriage vows to your lawful lord?"

I thought she might be angry, but she just sighed. "Understand me, stranger. Those were his words, not mine. For years, I have put it off. I heard of the destruction of Troy and the return of the other Greek warriors, but kept waiting. For years upon years, I have waited. It shames me to say that I tried to keep my own son from growing up, hoping to avoid the day. Finally, hounded beyond belief by the men you see here, I promised to remarry."

"You surprise me, my lady," he said softly, but his shoulders had tensed. "Would your husband Odysseus abandon his vows so easily?"

"Remember under whose roof you are a guest, stranger," she replied sharply. "I asked for your advice, not your reproof."

"Forgive me, my lady."

She gazed into the fire. "No, you are right," she said eventually. "If there were only me, I would act differently. But I must think of my son." She gestured around the room and toward one end, where the cockfight was over. Several suitors were chopping up a table for a fire to roast the dead roosters, lying in a heap nearby. The survivor strutted about the floor, preening its bloodied feathers.

"If I take a husband, he will force the rest of these men to leave. And my son Telemachus will still have an estate to inherit."

"Can you not delay them? Lead them on, but avoid promises? A child's game, for a woman such as you."

She glanced at him. "Stranger, how I tried. When they would no longer settle for refusal, I promised to take a new husband from among them, but only once I had finished weaving a burial shroud for my father-in-law."

The stranger nodded. "I understand. But somehow the shroud was never quite finished."

She looked at him shrewdly. "How fortunate that you were not among the suitors, stranger. On the largest loom I had, I began a burial shroud that would have fitted a brace of Titans. When it was half complete, I began unpicking the day's work each night, weaving in a different pattern the next day. Not being familiar with the womanly arts, and without much perception between them, the suitors accepted that the work continued."

"A clever ruse, my lady," said the stranger.

"Not clever enough, I fear," she replied. "It worked for many months, until one of my own maids betrayed me to her lover, the suitor Amphinomus. They burst in and caught me at it that same night, and forced a promise from me: I would marry in a month, or as soon as my son returned from Pylos."

She smiled sadly. "He has returned. And it seems he has met my husband's condition of adulthood too. Seeing him this morning, it seems clear that he is no longer a child."

"My lady," said the stranger, "I urge that you not be hasty. It is my belief that your husband is closer than you think." He leaned toward her. "*Much* closer. Even now he may be hatching plans to rid you of your suitors."

She turned and looked closely at his profile in the firelight. When she spoke, there was a catch in her throat. "Stranger, you don't know how much I want to believe you. But I've been deceived too often these last ten years, by men who claimed to know of my husband."

She glanced over at the suitors. "So now I must choose a

husband from among them, unpleasant though they are. A kingdom must have a king. The question now is who to choose."

The stranger shook his head slowly. "My lady," he said quietly, "none of these men is fit to wash your feet, let alone to win your hand." He gazed into the fire. "Permit me to suggest a contest. Something to separate the kids from the goats. A task that your husband could have performed easily, but one that would defeat lesser men."

She said nothing, lost in thought.

"Perhaps something involving archery," he added carefully.

She turned toward him. "Archery," she said slowly. "My husband used to stand some axes in a line, just outside these doors in the earth of the outer courtyard. Then with his favourite bow, he would shoot a single arrow through the chinholes of them all."

She smiled indulgently. "The arrows stuck in the far wall. If you look, you can still see the marks. Ten axes, as I recall." She looked closely at the stranger. "Is that the sort of thing you were thinking of?"

He returned her gaze for the first time. "Make it twelve, my lady."

She stared back. "Twelve?"

He nodded.

"Very well, stranger, if you think so. Twelve it is." She stood up. "Thank you."

Puzzled, I watched her stride off. Somehow I felt as though

I had just witnessed two conversations, the second of which I had seen, but not heard.

A moment later her voice rang across the room. "Suitors!" she called loudly.

I turned to see her speaking from the second floor balcony. "As you know," she went on, "I have promised to remarry. I hope you will pardon me for waiting so long. It was never my goal to frustrate you, but to wait until I was sure that my Odysseus was not coming back. After being married to such a man, I will settle for no one less."

She held up a hand for silence. "I declare a contest. My husband Odysseus was known to stand up a row of twelve axes and, with his great bow, shoot an arrow through the chin-holes of them all. The man who can do this is the man I will marry."

"Twelve axes?" someone said. "Impossible!"

She arched an eyebrow at him. "Perhaps for some, Amphinomus. But I assure you, my Odysseus never missed his target."

Telemachus stepped forward with the bow. The men fell silent. It was a thick-waisted, ugly thing, its black arch long and solid, the whipcord broken and re-knotted, the cruel-looking horns at either end curved sharply outward as if to snatch and pierce. "Tomorrow," he said, "we will hold the contest."

I had expected the men to celebrate, but the sight of the bow seemed to subdue them. They went to their beds early that night, without the evening's usual drunken antics.

I awoke the next morning to see Tel walking past, carrying a bundle of axes. "Hi, Theo," he said. "I'm sorry I haven't been a proper host. Things are unsettled right now. But that's all about to change." He glanced around the room and saw the stranger, still sitting by the fire, who caught his look and returned a courteous nod.

"Give me a hand," he went on. "Look through the holes and tell me when they're lined up." There it was again, a confidence he hadn't had two days earlier.

He led me out through the main doors of the room into the courtyard beyond. Marking out a trench with his foot, he sank the handle of each axe into it, standing it upright and tamping the earth down around it, adjusting each one to my gestures until it lined up with the others.

I took a closer look. Unlike the brutish, solid things carried by the guards at Mycenae and Sparta, these axes seemed to be almost for decoration. The axe head was formed with an ornamental curl that extended the cutting edge both above and below, like breaking waves. The curl below extended almost back to the handle, like a man's beard curving down and back toward his neck, resulting in a hole framed by the axe head, the handle and the ornamental strip. It was clear why Penelope had called them "chin holes."

"Looks easy, doesn't it, lad?" asked one of the suitors, an older man with a patch over one eye, coming up behind me.

I shrugged. "I guess so."

"Well, you'd guess wrong, then. It's near impossible, even

for men with two good eyes." He spat angrily into the dirt of the courtyard. "And she knows it, too, curse her. I doubt there's a man here who can do it."

He caught my look. "Don't believe me? Come here." He led me through the courtyard to the first axe.

"Look through, lad. It's not the shooting straight — any hamfist can do that with a bit of practice — it's shooting straight *and hard*. See, an arrow will fall as it flies, same as if you'd dropped it. An archer aims upward to get distance, but try that here and you'll miss the whole lot. So you've got to shoot your dead hardest to keep the arrow flying straight through all the holes. The archer who can shoot that hard *and* keep his aim, while crouching to get through those low holes — well, he deserves to win, I'll say that."

I looked at the row of axes with new respect. A contest that was deceptively simple, yet unexpectedly hard. The sort of thing my old master Odysseus might have come up with, if he'd still been alive.

"Honoured guests!" Telemachus was speaking from part way up the stairs, holding the nasty-looking bow in both hands. "We will now hold the contest. The man who is the most capable of stringing this, my father's bow, and sending an arrow through the chin-holes of the twelve axes out in the courtyard with a single shot, is the man my mother consents to marry."

He came the rest of the way down the steps and leaned the bow up against the door frame. "My father's arrows, I'm told, sank deep into the opposite wall of the courtyard, but my mother assures me that she will not hold you to the same standard. The arrow need only pass through all of the chin-holes."

There was a pause, and one of the suitors strode forward. "Let's have it," he said. "We can settle this quickly."

"Leiodes," said Telemachus calmly. "Here is the bow. Show us all how to do it."

One end of the bow string was permanently tied to one horn of the bow, while the other had a loop to snag around the other horn. Bows, I had learned on board the *Arethusa*, were normally stored unstrung to keep their spring, and strung again before each use. With one end of the bow on the floor, Leiodes pulled the other end of the bow down to loop the bowstring over it. Or at least, he tried to.

The bow didn't budge.

Surprised, he applied more weight, with the same result. Scowling, he shifted his weight and tried a third time. This time the bow flexed very slightly, but even with his muscles straining, he couldn't bring the bowstring loop anywhere near the horn. He struggled, bringing the horn and loop a little closer, but eventually gasped and let go.

"Give it here. Let a real man try," said one of the other suitors, reaching for the bow. Leiodes thrust it at him with a curse. The second man was taller and heavier, but fared even worse.

I watched for a little while but the men were having no

luck, some giving up quickly, others straining until someone pushed them aside, to loud catcalls from the others. If any of them managed to string the bow, I'd hear it, so I got up to take a walk around.

It was then that I noticed something strange: all of the weapons were gone from the walls. As I wandered around the room, examining the lighter patches where the shields and spears had hung, I discovered that the doors into the room had been shut, and been bolted from the outside, leaving open only the main double doors at the far end of the hall. I frowned as I noticed something else. Around the room, the pitchers and trays were sitting abandoned on tables. The slave girls who usually carried them had disappeared, vanishing like birds before a storm.

I wandered uneasily back toward the suitors. One of them was warming the bow over a fire while the others watched. "Of course," someone was saying. "It's Apollo's feast day. No wonder we're all having such miserable luck." I couldn't see the connection, but the other men were convinced.

"Well, there you go," the man holding the bow said, laying it down. "Eyeless fools we are, holding a contest like this on the Apollonian Feast. Let's give it another shot tomorrow. For now, a drink! Say, what happened to those serving wenches?"

The old beggar suddenly stepped forward, hunched over and leaning heavily on his staff. "If you young lords here have done your best," he said, his voice creaking with age, "perhaps I will give this contest a try."

Antin shot to his feet. "You? Be serious, old man. You can't lift it, let alone string it."

The beggar continued toward the bow, his staff tapping on the floor.

"Did you hear me, old man?" Antin shouted. "Or are you deaf as well as crippled? This contest is none of your concern. You mock the rest of us by trying."

The beggar had reached the bow. "Do I, my lord?" he replied. "Perhaps my lords will enjoy the sight of an old man trying something beyond the reach of his years."

"Give it a rest, Antin," someone called out. "The old fool should be good for a laugh."

Leaning heavily on his staff, the old beggar bent down and picked up the bow, to jeers from the suitors. As he straightened up, the hood slipped slightly and I caught his face in profile once again. He reminded me of someone. It felt terribly important that I remember who.

There was a dismayed murmur from the audience. The beggar had seated himself on a stool and was examining the bow carefully, turning it expertly in his hands as though testing its quality. At some point in his life he'd seen service as a bowman.

He stood up again slowly, leaning on his staff. This time the murmur sounded relaxed. The old fool might know how to handle a bow, it seemed to say, but the brute strength to string it, let alone draw it, was another matter.

Instead of stepping on one tip of the bow and trying to

pull the other tip down as the suitors had done, the beggar walked over and stopped at a spot where the floor tiles had shifted, creating a raised lip a few paces from the wall. The jeers of the suitors fell silent as he pushed one tip of the bow down into the raised tile lip and braced his foot against the wall. Stooping further, he put his shoulder against the upper tip of the bow and heaved. The bow flexed and he slipped the bowstring into place. He wasn't even breathing hard.

Half a dozen suitors were instantly on their feet. "How did you do that? It's a trick!" But the man with the eye-patch chuckled. "Sit down, the lot of you. He got us fair. Any one of us could have gone and found that spot, but we were too busy standing up and showing off."

"How did he know that floor patch was there?" someone asked, but was ignored. The beggar had picked up the quiver of arrows and was counting them carefully.

"Count well, old man," someone called. "It'll take you every arrow in that quiver to win this contest."

The beggar looked at him expressionlessly. "Of that I have no doubt." Kneeling, he plucked an arrow from the quiver, notched it onto the string and drew the bowstring back slowly. The room fell silent as he stood motionless, holding the bowstring at full extension.

"Shoot, old man!" someone called. As if he'd been waiting for it, he released the bowstring. The arrow whipped through the line of axes almost too fast to see, sinking half its shaft length into the far wall.

This time all the suitors were on their feet in the same instant. "Liar! Cheat!" voices were shouting. "It's a set-up! He missed!"

Antinous was the loudest. "What filthy trick is this?" he demanded, waving his knife. "Show us what you did, you little weasel, or I'll cut out your eyes."

The beggar looked around. "Good my lords, surely you don't think that a miserable beggar can fool such men as you? In that case, I will do it again. Antinous, step into the court-yard. Put your head down close to watch. When I am done, I swear that you shall have no doubt."

Antinous walked stiffly into the courtyard and knelt beside the last axe, his eyes narrowed. The beggar notched a second arrow to his string, drew and fired, but at the last instant shifted his aim almost imperceptibly to the left.

The arrow missed the axes entirely, buzzed through the air beside them and struck Antinous in the throat, moving with such speed that *it shot out the other side of his neck*, burying its head in the wooden wall behind him. Antinous brought his hands up to his throat, gurgled blood, staggered and collapsed.

There was an instant of silence, and every man in the room began shouting at once. "Clumsy idiot, you've shot him! For the sake of the gods, someone take that bow from him before he hits someone else! Then we'll cut the hands off the old fool!"

I watched from the sidelines, struggling to recall. Antinous's death was no loss. But where had I seen that manoeuvre before?

With the sudden, startling agility of a gazelle, the old beggar threw off his rags and leapt up on a heavy wooden table against the wall by the door. I gasped. His body was powerfully muscled, his shoulders broad, his skin etched but smooth. This was no old man.

"You think this was an accident?" he shouted as he snatched up the quiver, his voice suddenly stripped of its age. "Then let us see if I can do it again!" His hands moving almost too fast to see, he whipped three arrows out of the quiver and fired them, one after the other, into the crowd. Each one found its target, sinking into the head or chest of one of the suitors. The men surged back as if fleeing an inferno. Afraid to draw attention to myself, I stayed where I was, off to the side.

"Accident? I'm your accident, all right!" he shouted, his voice crackling with cold fury. "I'm Odysseus, home from Troy!"

I felt the blood drain from my face. My old master! Did he know me? Would he shoot me too, or protect me? I wasn't even sure I wanted him to win. Back when I had been a slave, I had come to see him as a friend, until he had given me away in a moment of anger. But having heard the suitors plotting, I was certain I wanted them to lose.

I didn't know what I should do. With no armour or weapons, it would be suicidal for me to face trained warriors. On the other hand, what would Odysseus do with me if he won and I hadn't helped? And what if he lost? The suitors would kill Telemachus to stop him from avenging his father, and me as his friend.

"Up-end the tables!" someone was shouting. Pursued by Odysseus's merciless arrows, the suitors had stampeded to the opposite end of the *megaron*, and now, clustered at the far end of the room, they were scrambling to turn the dining tables onto their sides as shields. There were at least twenty men lying dead or dying, and every arrow from Odysseus's bow took down another. With the other doors bolted, the only exit was through the main doors, and to pass through them meant getting past Odysseus and his bow.

The suitors knew it too. With the tables to protect them, they began to creep up from the far end of the room. Odysseus stood, his bowstring twanging at the glimpse of an arm or a head. "Suitors!" he shouted. "You despoiled my house and conspired to replace me in my own bed. Even then, I might have let you live. But then you contrived to kill my son. I hope you dined well, for your next meal will be in Hades!"

His position on the table was badly exposed. They were in disarray now, but as soon as the suitors organized themselves, they would rush him, carrying the tables as shields. Once within sword range, they could cut him to shreds.

He had to know it too, but his stance showed no uncertainty. As if he could tell I was watching him, he turned his head to the side momentarily, and one eyelid pinched shut, just for an instant. He knew me! At his glance, the warmth I had once felt for him came flooding back, and suddenly I knew whose side I had always been on.

His discarded staff was on the floor not far from me, and I

crept over to pick it up. It wouldn't be much use against swords, but I was no longer defenceless. I moved over to stand near the table Odysseus was perched on, still unsure of how I could help, but certain that I wanted to.

Three men in battle armour, equipped with swords and shields, came through the big doors behind Odysseus. I thought for a moment that they were suitors until I recognized Telemachus and Eumaeus the stockman. Each of them dropped a fresh quiver of arrows at Odysseus's feet. Telemachus went back out and closed the doors behind him, while Eumaeus and the other man walked up toward the suitors, now sheltering behind tables.

Two against a hundred? I thought they were committing suicide, until I realized that their strategy wasn't to fight; it was to keep the suitors at their distance. And there was something else too. As they approached the nearest table, taking care to stay out of the line of fire, they grasped its two upper corners, tipped it over, and jumped back. The men hidden behind the table leapt up in surprise. Three arrows whizzed through the air, instantly taking them down.

At that moment, Telemachus emerged from the storeroom behind the suitors. The men at the back yelped and scrambled up as his sword slashed at them. His technique was unskilled, but it didn't matter. The moment a suitor exposed himself to Odysseus's bow, he was as good as dead. I watched, amazed, as the two field hands turned another table. Between the four of them, they were slowly winning a battle against a hundred men.

This whole battle, I realized, had been carefully planned. Lopex — Odysseus, I reminded myself again — must have revealed himself to his son and the field hands, who had prepared the room for a slaughter, removing the weapons and bolting the doors shut.

Telemachus had moved away from the storeroom, whose door was now hanging open. The suitors didn't take long to notice. Three of them, carrying a table for cover, made a break for the door, emerging with some of the shields and spears that had been taken down from the walls earlier.

The open storeroom was something Odysseus hadn't prepared for. Suitors were already darting in and out, collecting spears and shields. Many of them dropped as they exposed their backs to his arrows, but those who survived were coming out armed. Now facing men with shields and spears, Odysseus's three defenders were being forced to fall back.

There was a hurried conference between several of the suitors, and one broke away to approach Odysseus behind a shield from the storeroom. Taking care not to expose any part of himself, he threw out his sword, which landed with a clatter near my feet.

"Great Odysseus!" he shouted over the din. "Please listen to what I say!" The noise slackened slightly. "You are right to be angry. We have behaved disgracefully, violating *xenia*, forgetting our sacred obligations as guests. But the man who was your true enemy, Antinous, is dead, your arrow through his throat. It was he who wanted your lands and your wife."

Odysseus said nothing.

"I will lower my shield so you may recognize me," said the speaker, coming closer. "I am Eurymachus. We knew one another as boys, Odysseus. It is my hope that you will let me speak before you shoot me." The shield crept down, revealing the silver hair and face of one of the suitors.

I glanced up at Odysseus on the table near me. His bow, an arrow on the string, was trained on the man's face. He looked older, his face more careworn, but with the hood off, he still reminded me of my father.

"I know you, Eurymachus," he said. "Speak."

"I swear to you that we will make good everything we have destroyed, everything that we have eaten, every plate or goblet that has been harmed, we will repay ten times over."

Odysseus said nothing.

Encouraged, Eurymachus took another step forward. From my position to the side, I could just see his left arm, tucked up awkwardly behind his back. Facing him head on and blocked by the man's shield, Odysseus couldn't see it.

"And cattle," Eurymachus added. "Many cattle! Twenty strong bulls from each of us still alive, and twenty from the families of those who are not. And further, great Odysseus, we will pour gold and silver into your palace coffers until they can hold no more."

I watched closely. As he spoke, his arm was moving down and up behind his back. Once . . . twice . . .

I had it. *He was signalling.*

"Look out!"

"THROW!"

My cry of warning to Odysseus came at the same instant as Eurymachus's shout to the suitors. As ten spears leapt from the crowd, I sprang in front of Odysseus, bringing the staff up to block as I'd done on the road to Pylos. Swinging the staff in a fast arc, I knocked most of the spears off course, but the effort left me off balance. Two suitors, cannier than the rest, had held back their spears from the first volley and threw them now. I spun the staff and knocked one away, but the other, only partly deflected, bit deep into my shoulder. I collapsed, twisting in agony on the ground.

Furious, Eurymachus advanced on me, brandishing the knife that he had hidden behind his back. As he raised his arm, an arrow sliced through his wrist. He shouted in pain, dropping his shield, and a second arrow took him through the chest. He clawed at it for only an instant before collapsing nearby.

Overcome by pain, and weakening as my blood ran free, I only dimly sensed the battle's violent finale. Someone pulled out the spear and dragged me off to the side. I had a vague sense of Odysseus, picking up the fallen sword and charging into the fray like a rabid bear, hacking through shields, spears, and people. The three fighters followed, mopping up the trail of wounded behind him. As my consciousness ebbed, I could only dimly hear the screams as the last suitors were overcome. Finally, there came darkness, as my own wounds overwhelmed me.

CHAPTER ELEVEN

The Long Road Home

I AWOKE TO FIND myself lying on the floor, my head on a cushion. An old woman was leaning over me, binding the wound in my shoulder. "Hush, child," she said as I yelped in pain. "Many are laid out here who would be glad to feel pain again."

"Please," I said, "can you wash it out first? With a clean rag?" She looked surprised, but did as I asked. I'd survived the battle, and wasn't about to let Greek healing do what the spear had failed to.

Someone came over and stood by my head, looking down. "You've grown, boy," he said. It was Odysseus. "We'll speak later." He turned to someone beside him. "Bind him. I don't trust him not to run off." I was too weak to run anywhere, but someone tied my hands and feet, tightly but not painfully.

From beside me came another voice. It was Telemachus. "What's going on?" he asked. "Why did my father want you tied up?" His tone became suspicious. "What are you hiding?"

I turned my head to see Tel squatting against the wall beside me. There was no point pretending any longer. "I know your father."

"You do?" He paused. "Why didn't you say so?"

I hesitated. This wasn't going to be pleasant. "I sailed with your father when he came back from Troy. But not as a warrior. Your father enslaved me when the Greeks took Troy."

"Enslaved?" Tel's brow wrinkled in confusion.

I sighed. "I'm Trojan. My name's not Theo, it's Alexi. Short for Alexias."

Tel seemed to think about it. I had expected him to be angry, but his next question went off in another direction. "Why did you take his side in the fight? You must hate him."

"I did. For a long time, I hated all Greeks," I said. "But stuff like this" — I gestured around us at the dead and dying men — "made me realize something. We weren't the only losers from the Greek war. Sorry, the Trojan War, as you call it. You Greeks lost, just as much as we did."

Tel looked at me strangely. "Don't take this the wrong way, Th — Alexi — but we won. Our men came back with shiploads of treasure and slaves. Not my father, but when I went to Pylos and Sparta . . ."

I nodded. "I went to Sparta, and to Pylos, and Mycenae

and Delphi too. Did you notice all the empty farms? How the citadels are full of old men? How the seas are full of raiders?"

Tel frowned. "Sure, that's pretty bad. But what does it have to do with the war?"

I turned to face him, wincing as I moved my shoulder.

"Because you lost so many men in the war. Fighting-age men. Fathers. Now the young kids are growing up wild. The sea is thick with raiders. The roads are full of bandits. Kingdoms like yours are being pulled apart, fighting over who will be the next king. The priest at Delphi said it best. He said he hoped the war had been worth it, because it had lost the Greeks your soul."

A noise nearby made me look up. A fine-boned young man was on his knees, hugging Odysseus around the legs and weeping. "Please!" he was saying. "I wasn't with them. They dragged me in here to sing for them. They kept me chained up. Please . . ."

Odysseus looked at him. "So sing, minstrel. Where's your lyre?"

The young man looked around desperately. "I think I lost it in the fight."

Odysseus, a knife in his other hand, grabbed the young man's hair and tipped his head back, a movement I'd seen all too often. "Wait!" I shouted. "That's Phemios the minstrel. I'm sure he's had no part in this."

Odysseus let go of the minstrel and walked over. "Alexias,

son of Aristides," he said, looking down at me. "I did you an injustice once by not listening to you, back on the isle of the winds. I don't make a mistake twice." He gestured at Phemios. "Go."

A ladylike cough from the direction of the stairs caught our attention. Penelope had come halfway down, stopping as she looked around at the carnage. Her eyes moved slowly over to Odysseus, whose body was glistening with sweat and blood.

"Do you know me yet?" he asked.

"You look like the man I used to call my husband," she replied carefully. "But I've been hoping for too long to believe anything."

Tel got to his feet. "Look around, mother! Do you know anyone else who could have done this?"

Odysseus spoke up. "It's okay, Tel. Your mother's a practical woman. It's just one of the reasons I love her. She'll know me by what I know. Meanwhile, I can sleep alone for a few more nights."

Penelope stirred herself as if from a dream. "Sleep. Yes. Clea, the stranger will need a bed this evening. Please fetch the bed from my room and put it in the spare room at the end of the hall."

The maid looked uncertainly at her. "Mistress?" she began.

Odysseus laughed. "It's okay, Euryclea. She's not asking much. Just to move the big double bed that was hers and mine every night until I went off to Troy. The one I carved myself from the olive tree I built this palace around. Here, take my sword. You'll need it to hack through the roots of the tree I carved it from, and to widen the doorway to let it through. I built the room around that bed, and the palace around the bedroom. Be careful not to disturb the gold and silver inlays that I built into the headboard. And don't touch the secret compartment on Penelope's side; she's always kept her best jewellery there, including the little brooch of the two dolphins that I gave her as a wedding present."

Overcome, Penelope opened her mouth but could get nothing out.

"Oh, and one other thing," Odysseus added. "You'd better pray for a lot of divine help, because no mortal person could do what she's asking." He broke off and looked at his wife. "Is that what you wanted, my dear?"

Penelope gave a sob and rushed the rest of the way down the stairs to throw herself into his arms, oblivious to the blood and sweat that coated him. "My dearest, dearest love," she murmured. "I was afraid you were never coming home."

"Did I not say I would?" he replied, gazing at her fondly.

Their embrace was so long that we looked away in embarrassment. Finally, Odysseus turned to me. "As for you, Alexi, your master Ury is dead. By law, his property reverts to me." He shook his head. "He was right about you, back in Troy. You're too independent to make a good slave. There's only one thing I can do." He took out his knife.

"Father!" Telemachus blurted, grabbing his father's arm. "He saved your life!"

Odysseus knelt beside me and sliced easily through the ropes binding my hands and feet. "Did you think I was going to kill him?" he asked, looking at Telemachus. "You don't know me very well, do you, my son?" He smiled slightly. "I suppose that's my fault. But we'll start fixing that today."

He got to his feet. "Alexi, you have served me well. You're welcome to stay in my house, or what's left of it, for as long as you like. Not as a slave or even a servant, but as a guest, equal in status to my own son."

I swallowed. "Thank you, mast — I mean, thank you. May I ask you something?"

"Of course."

"The shipwreck. How did you survive?"

His face seemed to sag. "All my men, lost, but for the two of us. Athene must have favoured me, as she has so often done. I clung to a piece of wreckage, drifting to the island of Calypso, the nymph. She kept me as a . . . prisoner." He glanced sidelong at his wife, who was listening with interest.

"At last she freed me. I built a raft and sailed to the land of the Phaecians, where King Alcinous dwells. He welcomed me and offered me a ship to take me home." He turned to his wife. "To you, my dear wife, at long last."

"How dull it must have been, imprisoned by this nymph," she remarked sympathetically. "But I'm sure you found ways to keep busy, my dear. Men always do."

Odysseus looked back at me. "And you, Alexi," he asked quickly. "What are your plans?"

I shrugged. "I've spent years searching for Trojan survivors of the war, looking for news of my sister, but I've failed. Ithaca was my last hope."

Tel spoke up. "You're looking for Trojans? That's strange." He turned to Odysseus. "It was while I was out looking for news of you, father. I had set out for Pylos but a wind came up and blew us west, off course. We landed on an island off Dalmatia. The locals call it Proat. We found a colony of Trojans there who had escaped the war. Mostly women."

Hope fluttered in my chest. "Go on. Please."

Telemachus looked surprised at my anxious tone. "Well, we'd been there for ten days, repairing some storm damage and refilling our cistern. The repairs took awhile. Something to do with being on an island of women, I think. The sailors were in no hurry."

Neither was he. "So . . ." I prompted him.

"So the last night there, the woman who seemed to be in charge of the settlement invited us to a feast. They passed around some wine. I guess I drank a little too much." He blushed. "She was gorgeous! Tall and slender. Black hair and grey eyes. A lot like yours, Alexi, but they looked better on her."

He caught my impatient glare. "Sorry. Anyway, as I said, I drank too much. I guess I was trying to impress her. I told her that my father was Odysseus, hero of the Trojan War." He shook his head. "Bad move. Really bad move! I guess she sees the Trojan War a bit differently.

"The evening ended right there. She set her dogs on us! It

was all we could do to get back to the ship. And when we got to the beach, their warriors had been alerted. All women, but as fierce as leopards. We barely got aboard." He shook his head sadly. "It's too bad. I'd really like to have seen her again."

I couldn't stand it anymore. "Her name!" I shouted, struggling to sit up. "What was her name?"

He looked at me, surprised. "Didn't I say? She called herself Melantha."

I sagged back onto the cushion. Melantha. Could it be true? It was a common enough name. And some with it were bound to be tall and slender. And a few of those would have black hair and grey eyes. But how many could be all that and Trojan too?

I looked up at Odysseus, who was standing still as Penelope and the old nurse sponged off the blood and sweat that covered him. "Sir?" I asked. "May I borrow a ship and a crew?"

"Of course. Telemachus, go with him. Use the ship you took to Pylos."

Telemachus opened his mouth to say something, but caught his father's eye and shut it again.

I nodded gratefully. "As soon as I can, if possible."

Odysseus glanced at my shoulder, now bound up with a cloth, but said simply, "As you wish. And let me add to that some advice. This young lady who has caught your attention, she may not know you anymore. You've changed. Or she may have moved on." He looked at his wife. "Give her time to know you again."

I'd been afraid the voyage would be slow, but as soon as we set sail the next morning, it began to feel too fast. What if it wasn't her? What if she resented me for leaving her to the Greeks? Anything might have happened to her since that night in Troy. By the time the lookout spotted the island of Proat, four days out of Ithaca, I was too anxious to sleep.

There was no wharf, so we pulled up on a pebbly beach below the town. Tel and I went alone through the winding dirt streets of the settlement, leaving the crew behind to make our peaceful intentions clear.

"I don't know about this, Alexi," Tel said nervously. "What if she recognizes me? She set the dogs on me last time, you know." Separated from his father, he sounded a lot more like the Telemachus I'd first met on the Pylos road.

He wasn't the only anxious one. As he stopped in front of a small wooden building, I felt a rush of panic. "Tel," I said quickly. "Wait."

He turned.

"I don't think I can do this."

He peered at me. "What do you mean? Don't you want to see her?"

"What if she isn't *her*? What if she hates me?" I could feel my heart racing. "You go. Show her this." I fumbled the knife Kassander had returned to me from its loop in my chiton.

Tel took it gingerly. "What is it?"

"It's my knife. Well, hers. See if she recognizes it. I'll wait outside."

I ducked out of sight as he climbed the stone steps to the

main entrance, a simple wooden door on two bronze hinges.

"I'm sorry to disturb you. I'm looking for Melantha," I heard him say, sounding hesitant. Someone asked him in and the door closed. I crept back and stood near the open window. I could just make out voices.

"Do I know you?" someone asked. A woman's voice. Too soft to tell whose it was.

Tel began to stammer. "Me? No, I don't see how. It's not like I've been here before." Apparently he hadn't inherited his father's skill at lying.

"I *do* know you," came the woman's voice, sounding suspicious. "You're the son of that Greek bandit." Her voice hardened. "You've got to the count of three to explain what you're doing here. One, two . . ."

"Wait!" said Tel. "Look at this!"

"What's that to me?" the woman's voice began, but broke off with a gasp. "*Where did you get this?*" There was a thump, followed by a yelp of pain.

I pushed the door open and dashed in. Tel was on his stomach on the floor of a small greeting room, a tall, black-haired woman kneeling on his back, holding Mela's knife to his throat. How had she done that so quickly? I touched her shoulder without thinking. She spun around instantly, grabbing me by the hair and throwing me face first against the wooden floor beside Tel before I could back away. Her knee ground into my back.

"Move and die, Greeks," she barked. "Guards!"

I struggled to sit up and turn around, but her knife point

was at the side of my neck instantly. "Melantha!" I shouted, as several female guards rushed into the room. "It's me! Alexi!"

The knife pressure slackened. "Alexi?"

"Let me up. You'll see."

The knee came off my back. I got to my knees and slowly turned around.

Behind me stood a tall, grey-eyed woman with straight black hair like mine, flanked by three female guards. She was a little older and more battle-wearied, but there was no doubt who she was.

"Alexi?" she repeated, frowning.

I nodded.

She stared at me. "All right, prove it."

I nodded at the knife in her hand. "Father gave you that when you turned thirteen. A coming-of-age gift. Mother couldn't present it because she died when I was a baby."

Her gaze went to me, then to the knife, and returned at last to me. "Alexi . . ."

I nodded again. Suddenly we were hugging fiercely. "I thought you were dead, Alexi," she was saying.

"I thought you were too," I said, blinking hard. "But you weren't in Hades, so I knew you'd survived."

She pulled back, startled. "Hades?"

I hesitated. "It's a long story. Okay, a very long story."

"Good." She turned to the guards. "Please ask the kitchen to prepare a banquet for tonight, and some wine for now." She turned back to me. "I want to hear it all."

Tel stood up carefully. "Melantha," I said, "let me introduce my friend Telemachus of Ithaca. Son of Odysseus, a hero of the Greek war, but don't hold that against him. He's very nice."

Telemachus bowed with unexpected grace. "My lady."

My sister blushed. "I'm sorry about pinning you," she said, nodding toward the floor. "Are you all right?"

Tel smiled. Quite a charming smile, now that I noticed. And he was the son of a king. A good match for any woman.

"Don't mention it," he said. "I'm sorry I didn't bring a guest-gift for you."

She looked from him to me and laughed, a sound I had missed more than I'd realized. "You've brought me back my family. I can't imagine a better gift than that."

She hugged me again. "I want to hear everything that's happened, and I don't care how long it takes."

She turned and looked Telemachus up and down carefully. "As for you, Telemachus, son of Odysseus, you may stay as long as you like, in spite of your father."

Tel returned her gaze. "I was hoping you'd say that. I want to hear everything that my father's been up to. You do know he's been away since I was born, don't you? The truth is, I don't even know him."

Mela reached out and took my hand. "Until now, I had never thought that anything good came out of that war." She reached her other hand out to Telemachus, who took it gingerly. "Perhaps I was wrong."

WORDS THAT MAY PUZZLE YOU

We don't know that much about the language of Bronze-Age Greece. In 1200 BCE, the time of the Trojan War, what we think of as ancient Greece was still centuries in the future. Although Homer shows the Greeks and Trojans speaking to each other on the battlefield, the Trojans most likely spoke a different language. I've called it Anatolean, after the region, but nobody knows for sure.

Throughout the book, I've used classical Greek words and expressions. Who knows? Perhaps the same expressions were also popular five hundred years before, during the Trojan War. Here are some that you may have wondered about:

Akonitos: Aconite. Poisonous root of plants in the monk's-hood family.

Amphora: A large urn with two handles for carrying and pouring liquids. Smaller than a *pithos*.

Arachnios: A nickname Alexi creates from the Greek *arachne*, which means spiderweb, and was also the girl in the famous story of the weaving contest, which Alexi would certainly have known.

Archon: Ruler.

Basternion: A litter, or ornate chair on a platform carried by slaves. Reserved for the rich and powerful.

Chiton: A man's tunic.

Eksepsis: Blood poisoning. The English word "sepsis" comes from the same root.

Gloutos: Buttocks.

Hagios: A Greek condition meaning, approximately, "protected by the gods." The best English equivalent might be "sanctified."

Hand: A unit of time, slightly longer than an hour. We don't know how the Bronze-Age Greeks measured time, but there are other cultures who have used units equal to the length of time the sun takes to pass behind an outstretched hand, from wrist to fingertips. Perhaps Bronze-Age Greeks did the same.

Himation: A garment, more like a cloak, probably worn overtop something like a *chiton*.

Houmos: Hummus, the middle-eastern garlic and chickpea dip. Probably not an authentic ancient Greek word.

Khalash: No meaning. Just something the Cicones said when they stabbed someone. An English translation might be "Yahoo!" or perhaps "Take that, you *kopros sniffer!*"

Koprolith: A fossilized or otherwise petrified piece of *kopros*. Source of the English word *coprolith*.

Kopros: Ahem. Dung.

Koprophage: Someone who eats *kopros*.

Koprophile: Someone who loves *kopros*.

Kottabos: A Greek drinking game that involved flicking drops of wine from their goblet at a target.

Kuna: A word with a variety of meanings, one of which is (only literally) a female dog.

Kylix: A wide-mouthed, shallow drinking goblet.

Krater: A large vessel for mixing water and wine. About the size of a punch bowl.

Lawagetas: A mid-level military commander.

Lotos: Untranslated. Homer refers to the "lotos-eaters," from which we get the modern term "lotus eaters." He describes the lotus as a "flowery fruit" but gives us no other clues about what it might be. The seed pod of the opium poppy, from which we also make heroin, could be called that.

Megaron: The long central room in ancient Greek houses and palaces, often with pillars lining the two long walls. There would usually be a raised hearth in the centre.

Methusai: Drunken women. An insult, especially when applied to men.

Nekros: A corpse.

Nothos: A person of no legitimate family, or more specifically, of unknown father. An insult.

Ophion: Opium. Not clear that this word is authentic. Also means *serpent*.

Pelagios: The name — at least in this version — of Odysseus's ship.

Pestillos: Pestle, as in "mortar and." Probably not authentic.

Pithos: A large urn with a wide mouth for transporting liquids and grains.

Rhyton: A cone-shaped cup or glass, often with a hole at the bottom from which you could pour wine or liquid directly into your mouth.

Sakcharis, Sakchar: Sugar. It's unlikely that the Greeks had the granulated white form that we're used to.

Skatophage: An eater of *skatos*.

Skatos: Also known as *kopros*.

Stratiotai: One of a wide range of Greek words used for soldier.

Suagroi: Wild pigs.

Sueios ekpneusis: Literally, bad smelling gas from a pig.

Sueromenoi: People with a romantic attachment to pigs. Singular would be *sueromenos*.

Troglos: Short form for the ancient Greek *troglodytos*, or cave dweller.

Xeneon: The guest room of a house. Since there were no hospitals, a doctor would examine or operate on you in his *xeneon*. Ancient Greeks didn't do many operations, but they did do amputations. The stumps were probably sealed and disinfected by cauterizing them with a burning torch. Your chances of survival weren't that high.

Xenia, Xenios: The ancient Greek concept of what was called the host-guest relationship, specifically, the honour associated with fulfilling your role correctly as host or guest. This normally involved giving gifts. Especially amongst high-born families, giving such gifts was as much a source of honour as receiving them.

AFTERWORD

Writing these books has been one of the most enjoyable things I have ever done. Once *Torn from Troy* was published, I discovered that authors also get asked to visit schools. Who knew? Nonetheless I'm delighted, because talking to students throughout Canada about Greek mythology and my books, listening to their ideas and answering their questions turns out to be every bit as much fun as writing the books themselves has been.

I am often asked "Was there really a Trojan War?" Nobody knows for sure. Most authorities agree that there was some sort of war between the city-state of Troy and some of the Greek-speaking peoples. Archaeological evidence at the site of Troy certainly suggests it was destroyed by war, although there are many "layers," as the city was probably rebuilt many times after natural disasters, wars or other causes of destruction. With ancient cities, this is more common than you might think.

Was there a Trojan Horse? Wouldn't it be amazing if there were? There's no proof any longer. Made of wood, it would have rotted away thousands of years ago. Many scholars think it never existed, but others think it might have been an early type of siege tower, a fortified tower that was rolled up to the city walls to let the attackers climb without being exposed on ladders. Nearly everything else that Homer wrote that archaeologists can check (names and locations of cities, for example) has turned out to be accurate; perhaps this was too. Whether there was a Trojan Horse or not, it's easily the most compelling story in all of classical mythology.

A second question I am asked is how closely I've stuck to Homer's original *Odyssey*. That's a hard one. I've tried hard not to contradict anything Homer put into the *Odyssey*, but I've felt free to add plenty of details he left out. He doesn't mention slaves at all, for instance, let alone someone named Alexi. But even staying true to what's in the *Odyssey* has often been a challenge. For example, he says that Odysseus "shot an arrow through twelve axes." Seriously? Maybe with a titanium arrowhead and tin foil axes; otherwise, that just couldn't work. Many scholars over the centuries have tried to figure out what Homer really meant. I chose the option that seemed the most plausible. But, not counting a few exceptions and interpretations like that, what I've written remains true to Homer's original story — or at least doesn't contradict it too much.

The ancient Greece that most of us think of is what historians call "Classical Greece" — the period of Greece's great cultural achievements, including most of its plays and works of philosophy. This period, plus its build-up and decline, ran from about 750 BCE to 200 BCE, with its height from about 500 BCE to 300 BCE. But there is another period of Greek history — the "Age of Heroes," as the Greeks called it — that came earlier. This was the age of Perseus, Jason and the Argonauts. And of Odysseus, Achilles, Hector, and the other heroes of the Trojan War. It was a time that the Greek gods walked the earth with humans and interfered in their affairs, something the

Greeks of the later classical era generally agreed didn't happen any longer.

As a mythical era, it doesn't have real dates, but the ancient Greeks believed it ended right around the Trojan War. Greeks in the classical era looked back on this mythical age of heroes the way we look back on the era of Robin Hood and Merlin — a strange, legendary period when magic was still real. But with one difference: for the Greeks, the age of heroes really happened. Doubting the Trojan War, or the adventures of Hercules, would have been like doubting the battle of Waterloo, or the American Revolution. The Greeks believed that the heroes who conquered Troy really existed. In contrast, Greek gods didn't demand that you believe in them, so long as you kept up your sacrifices.

Shortly after the end of the Trojan War — dated by most scholars to around 1200 BCE, or 1184 BCE for the really confident — Greek civilization went into a decline, very much like the European dark ages. The main citadels of Greece, including Mycenae, were destroyed or abandoned during that time and never rebuilt. Nobody knows why. Explanations range from overgrazing by goats (I'm not making that up), to a massive drought, to attacks by the mysterious "Sea People," although nobody is clear about who they might have been. It took around four hundred years before Greek civilization escaped its dark ages and the classical era began. So for four hundred years, the stories of the Trojan War were passed down by storytellers around cooking fires at night, before they were finally written down around 750 BCE. How much did that change them? Nobody knows that either.

Because of the uncertainties about the Trojan War, most scholars have ignored the fact that the Greek dark ages began right around the time that the Trojan War ended. Ah, but what if it wasn't a coincidence? What if the Trojan War actually *caused* the Greek dark ages?

I want to thank my sister Laurel, a professor of Greek and Roman history, for this remarkable insight. But as she points out, if you read carefully, it's all there in Homer. Bless me, what *do* they teach them at these schools?

ABOUT THE AUTHOR

 Greek mythology has fascinated me since I discovered a copy of *Bulfinch's Mythology* in my father's library as a child. All the same, my writing career took a twenty-year detour through software development before I was able to become a full-time writer and spend more time at home raising my daughters, Kathleen and Anitra.

I started with Homer's *Odyssey* because it's a classic story, but one that nowadays is rarely read outside of university courses. I decided to create a version that young people would read for fun: a realistic adventure, as seen not through the eyes of the traditional Greek heroes, but from the perspective of an outsider. Because history is written by the victors, people have for centuries seen the destruction of Troy through the eyes of the Greeks. I felt it was time to see it through the eyes of a Trojan.

My family and I live in Toronto, where, at least until recently, the winters were growing steadily milder and the summers muggier. And at long last, we have a dog.

MARQUIS

Québec, Canada

RECYCLED
Paper made from
recycled material
FSC® C103567

Printed on Enviro 100% post-consumer EcoLogo certified paper,
processed chlorine free and manufactured using biogas energy.

    BIO GAS *ENERGY*